THE DEVIL STEER

"There!" Steven stood in the stirrups and pointed.

"In the clump of trees!"

I spotted him. Half-hidden among the olive trees, Diablo stood watching our every move. His left eye was missing. The other stared at us like a demon—the eye of the devil. With an angry toss of his head, the huge bull lumbered out onto the mesa like an army tank geared for combat.

"He's gonna do it," I said. "He's gonna take us on."

Our eyes were riveted on the approaching steer. Two hundred feet away Diablo stopped, raised his head and flared his nostrils as if to confirm a hated scent. Then the massive head lowered and, with a savage snort, he began to paw the ground, throwing dirt across his broad back and high into the air.

Like a sudden blow to the belly, reality struck me. This wasn't make-believe. In about twenty seconds, two thousand pounds of enraged bull would charge at us like a runaway freight tra

ONE LAST TIME

WILLIAM J. BUCHANAN

AN AVON FLARE BOOK

ONE LAST TIME is an original publication of Avon Books. This work has never before appeared in book form. This is a work of fiction, and while some portions of this novel deal with actual events and real people, it should in no way be construed as being factual.

AVON BOOKS
A division of
The Hearst Corporation
1350 Avenue of the Americas
New York, New York 10019

Copyright © 1992 by William J. Buchanan
Published by arrangement with the author
Library of Congress Catalog Card Number: 91-93004
ISBN: 0-380-76152-1
RL: 5.6

First Avon Flare Printing: February 1992

AVON FLARE TRADEMARK REG. U.S. PAT. OFF. AND IN OTHER COUNTRIES, MARCA REGISTRADA, HECHO EN U.S.A.

Printed in the U.S.A.

RA 10 9 8 7 6 5 4 3 2 1

For Steven

One Last Time is based on an actual event. I would like to thank my son, Steven, for his invaluable input to the story, and my daughter, Rebecca, for her help during the final preparation of the manuscript. In addition, I wish to acknowledge a debt of gratitude to my late friend, Linn ''Chad'' Zolman, for introducing me to the lore and lair of Diablo.

Chapter 1

From the time I was eight, it had been my chore to rise each morning at dawn to build the fires in the adobe ovens, where my mother baked bread for the pueblo store. Two of these smoke-blackened ovens were in the courtyard, just outside my bedroom window. They were fired every morning, except Sunday. It wasn't an unreasonable task. Still, for years I had looked forward to my fifteenth birthday when my younger brother, Miguel, would build the fires instead, and I would begin the work of a *vaquero* on the rangelands with my father.

On a chill March day, that long awaited birthday arrived. It turned out to be a day I would never forget.

That Saturday I awakened Miguel at first light. Half-asleep, he followed me into the kitchen. Our bowls and cups were already at our places on the bare pine table our grandfather had crafted from a high-country ponderosa fifty years before I was born. We pulled our chairs to the table and watched our mother prepare our breakfast on the electric stove she had insisted our father buy for her, despite criticism from the older women of the Pueblo. As always, she had the kitchen radio tuned to KHFM in Albuquerque. Mama liked long-hair music. As far as I was concerned, it was her only fault.

Mama wished me a happy birthday.

"Oh, yeah—" Miguel yawned long and hard. "Happy birthday from me too."

Though she wouldn't mention it until it was done, I knew that later that day Mama would use the electric oven to bake my favorite white cake with chocolate icing. The expectation made me happy. If only I could have persuaded her to bake the bread for the pueblo store in the electric oven. I could have slept later each morning. But she'd never do that.

My father's chair was empty.

"Where's Papa?" I kept my voice low, so not to awaken Grandpa Baca, whose room was just down the hall from the kitchen.

My mother turned off the burner and brought the pot to the table. "Tino came for him early. They've gone to the river." She shook my brother's shoulder. "Stay awake, Miguel." She ladled hot oatmeal into our bowls.

"The river?"

"Tino's pens were broken into last night. Two heifers missing."

I thought about that while I added milk and brown sugar to my oatmeal. "Diablo?" I asked.

She nodded. "They think he came down from the mountains after sundown." The concern in my voice hadn't escaped her. "Don't worry, David. Your father can take care of himself." I knew she was right, but I said a silent prayer anyway.

A half-hour later in the courtyard I showed Miguel how to use the axe to split the piñon logs, then how to load the ovens for maximum heat using the least wood. By the time the sun appeared above snow-capped Manzano Peak, high on the east mesa, the fires were set for another day. It was then that we saw Manuel Tome's blue Ford pickup raising a cloud of dust, as it raced down the dirt road that led to our house. Barely slowing for the narrow wooden bridge that spanned the irrigation ditch, Manuel sped on. He braked to a hard stop in our barren front yard, scattering a flock of panicky chickens.

"David!" Manuel yelled as he jumped from the cab. "Get your mother."

In the bed of the truck, with his head cradled on a folded saddle blanket, my father lay still as death. His face, deep-bronzed from a lifetime of riding beneath the fierce New Mexico sun, was now sickly pale. His eyes were closed. His best friend, Tino Valdez, was kneeling over him with a knee pressed into my father's groin. Beneath Tino's knee a pool of dark blood was clotting in the bed of the truck.

Stunned, I couldn't move.

"David!" Tino said, sharply, "Do as Manuel says. Now!"

I wheeled and ran toward the house. But my mother had already heard. Before I reached the porch she was out the door and down the steps. For a long moment she stared at my father's prostrate form.

"He was gored, Anna," Tino said. "Not as bad as it looks, I think."

Anna Chino was not of the Isleta people. A Mescalero Apache, at eighteen she won a beauty pageant scholarship to the University of New Mexico in Albuquerque. There she met my father, Ramon Baca, while he was performing in a rodeo at the state fair. A year later they were married in a tribal ceremony at the Mescalero reservation. That afternoon, at my mother's insistence, they repeated their vows before a priest in nearby Ruidoso. Though she moved to my father's home on the backside of Isleta Pueblo, and

3

adopted some Isleta ways, she would not abandon her strong-willed Apache heritage. On the day she came to Isleta she walked four miles to the 7-Eleven store in the village of Bosque Farms, just off the reservation. From there she called Mountain Bell and ordered a telephone to be installed in her new home. Then she called a contractor and arranged to have the house wired for electricity. A week later, with money she'd saved from a part-time job at the university, she bought a second-hand Chevy pickup truck for her personal use. At first, her independent ways made her something of a curiosity on the Pueblo. Nonetheless, from the beginning, the Isletans respected her. Some even admired her.

Now, she said, "Move your knee, Tino."

She worked her hand through the tear in my father's jeans and probed in and around the wound in his thigh. After a moment she withdrew her hand, stained now with my father's blood. "Bring him inside. I'll call Doctor Taub."

Within the hour a dozen other trucks, and at least that many saddled horses, filled our yard. Men, old and young, kept vigil outside the small adobe house. Miguel and I sat on the edge of the brick porch, anxious for news of what was happening to our father with the doctor inside. Tino Valdez sat with his back against an upright *viga*, assuring us that all would be well. With each newcomer, Tino was obliged to repeat the story.

"When we reached the cottonwood grove," Tino explained, "Ramon and I split up. Ramon suspected that Diablo hadn't returned to the mountains but had stayed in the lowlands. Just inside the mud flats we found fresh prints. Cloven—some huge, others smaller . . ."

4

"Diablo . . . with Tino's heifers," one of the men suggested.

Tino nodded. "We split up to search from different directions. I rode in from the north, Ramon from the south. We planned to meet again midway, then cross the river to search the other side. We believed that if we could flush Diablo into the open we could take him. We'd been parted . . . maybe ten minutes, when I heard Ramon cry out. I spurred hard. But by the time I found him, Ramon was already on the ground unconscious. He'd taken a horn in his thigh . . . here." Tino touched his own leg. "His horse was down, too— still alive, but with his belly ripped open. There was blood everywhere. I tied Ramon's belt high up around his leg to slow the bleeding and put him over my saddle. Then I got my rifle and ended his horse's agony. I mounted and rode fast to where I met Manuel in his truck at the cottonwood grove. He'd heard my shot and was coming to investigate. We put Ramon in the truck and brought him here."

There was a shaking of heads.

"Did you see the devil?" someone asked.

"No," Tino replied.

"He was lying in ambush," someone suggested.

"A sneak attack," said another.

"His way," said another.

"The only way Ramon could have been caught," said another.

"Yes, yes," they all agreed, nodding in unison.

The door opened and Doctor Taub emerged from the house with his bag in his hand. The gathered men looked at the young Anglo physician expectantly, but he motioned to Miguel and me and led us around the house away from the others. "The wound was deep, your father lost much blood."

Miguel grasped my hand. I gave his hand a reas-

5

suring squeeze. "He's gonna be all right, isn't he?" I asked.

"Oh . . . yes, yes," Doctor Taub assured us. "In time. There's no major arterial damage. The wound is closed. Your mother is a strong woman, David, a strong woman indeed. But for a while you're going to have to be the man here. You understand?"

"I . . . yes."

"Good . . . good. Now, both of you, go inside. I'll explain to the others."

Our father lay on the four-poster double bed where Miguel and I had been born. His head and back were propped high with pillows, his face was sallow. The patchwork quilt covering him rose and fell with the rhythm of his breathing. He was asleep. Near the bed, Grandpa Baca sat with his ancient eyes fixed on his son. Our mother was gathering the bloodied clothing from the floor and placing it in a wicker basket. When Miguel and I entered the room, she set the basket down and put her arms around our shoulders. "He's sedated. He'll sleep through the night." She hugged us tighter. "He's going to be all right." Her calm voice comforted us.

When she left to take the clothes to wash, Miguel went with her. I stood at the foot of the bed, gazing at my father's ashen face, my mind a jumble of emotions. Diablo had almost killed him. And my father was not the first. For years, angry voices on the Pueblo had called for Diablo to be shot on sight. But the pueblo council refused. The maverick bull would be dealt with only in the specific way they had approved. Many had tried. All had failed.

My anxiety turned to anger. In spite of the danger, the hunt had become a game. A game that only the *vaqueros* were allowed to play. A game from which I had been excluded because of my age. Well, today

6

I was fifteen. And the man lying there with his leg ripped open was my father. A plan began to take shape in my mind. I would avenge my father. And I'd do it the *vaquero* way, the way the pueblo council demanded it be done.

But I'd need help. And I knew exactly where to get it: From someone who had also met Diablo, face to face!

Chapter 2

First, I want to mention Steven.

"That gringo boy," my father called him, never mentioning him by name.

"*Anglo*," my mother would correct him, not always gently. "And his name is Steven."

"Hmmmph!" my father would snort.

Steven Callister was the son of none other than Jess Callister. It's a name that everyone should recall. For ten years, New Mexican Jess Callister was the champion rodeo cowboy in all the world. An international celebrity, he was renowned both in this country and in Europe, where he performed before royalty, and where anything to do with the American West was idolized. A photograph of him exchanging cowboy hats with President Reagan in the White House rose garden made the cover of *Western Horseman*. By the end of his reign, from which he retired undefeated, his lifetime earnings, including TV and magazine commercials, were right up there with the likes of Jim Shoulders and Larry Mahan. After leaving the circuit, he bought and restored a hundred year old, rambling adobe house on a four-hundred-acre spread of pasture land and cottonwood groves in the Rio Grande Valley, just across the river from Isleta Reservation. He fixed up the barns and corrals and set out to breed and train roping horses. The pride of his stock was the giant palomino stallion, Cheyenne, on which he'd won most of his trophies, and which he now put to stud. Cheyenne was the biggest horse anyone in the valley had ever seen. Rumors were that a breeder in Wyoming once offered a half-million dollars, cash on the barrel head, for the golden stallion. Jess Callister rejected the offer flat out. No one else would ever own Cheyenne, he proclaimed.

I learned most of this after I met Steven Callister. Here's how that happened.

At the end of my first day of school at Los Lunas High, I boarded the Bosque Farms school bus rather than the Isleta bus. The Bosque Farms bus stopped within walking distance of my home, and got there quicker. I'd no sooner settled onto the gaucho seat at the front of the bus when a dark shadow invaded my space. "Outa here, Chief. This bus ain't for injuns."

I didn't have to look up to know who that foghorn voice belonged to. Bobby "Bulldog" Jenkins was a jerk. He was bad news. Like me, he was a freshman. He'd been a freshman the year before, too. With the brain of a toad and the muscles of a gorilla, he earned his nickname by his ability to bulldog a thousand pound longhorn steer quicker than anyone else at Los Lunas High. 'Course, not many of us were stupid enough to try. In addition to throwing steers around, Bulldog compensated for dim wits by bullying everyone at the school, Indians and Mexicans preferred. Despite the fact that in the valley, *he* was in the ethnic minority, no one dared stand up to him. In the beginning a few tried, to their regret. No longer willing to risk having their faces rearranged, most guys went out of their way to avoid him.

9

When I didn't move quick enough to suit him, Bull-dog grabbed my arm, yanked me to my feet and stuck his blackhead-pitted face right in mine. "You're not listenin', Chief. I said, Outa here . . . *now*!"

"Aw, c'mon, Bulldog," one of the guys with him said, "cool it, huh?"

Bulldog gave the guy a look that would wither gran-ite. "Outa my face, Pea-Brain or you walk too."

The would-be peace maker retreated to the safety of a rear seat.

Although I was two-thirds Jenkins's size, and plenty scared, I'm no coward. I grabbed his wrist and tried to pry his hand from my arm. "Damn it, Bulldog . . . let me alone!"

Defiance didn't set well with him. "Who the hell you cussin' at, Injun?" He tightened his grip so hard I thought my arm would break. All I could do was stand there dumb and hurting, with tears of pain and humiliation welling in my eyes. Although by now the bus was full, no one else dared intervene. They knew that in a few more seconds I'd be pulp on the floor and there was nothing anyone could do about it.

Bulldog began to shake me. "I asked you a ques-tion, Injun. Who the hell you think you're cussin' at?"

At that moment a strange voice behind me spoke up cool as spring water: "Sounded pretty plain to me. He was cussin' at you . . . you bullying blockhead."

Leaden silence.

Bulldog released his grip on my arm so fast that I dropped like a brick into the seat. Bulldog stared in disbelief at the guy seated next to me. "Who . . . wha . . . ?" he sputtered. "Blockhead?!" He made a threatening move toward my seat-mate. "Who the hell you think you . . . ?"

The guy at my side stood up. He was an inch shorter than Bulldog, but every bit as brawny. He pushed a

10

gray sweat-stained Stetson to the back of his head but didn't say a word. Jaw set, fists clinched, he stared straight at Bulldog, and waited. For breathless seconds Bulldog met that steely gaze with one of his own. Then—I was close enough to see it—he blinked. Seeing something in those determined dark-brown eyes he didn't like, Bulldog took a step back. "Screw you, injun lover. I'll check you later." With that lingering threat, he joined a friend in a rear seat, and sat there fuming.

"Jesus!" I exclaimed when my seat-mate sat back down. "Nobody . . . I mean *nobody* ever backed that ape down before." I shoved my hand toward my benefactor. "I'm David . . . David Baca. Listen, thanks. Thanks one hell of a lot."

He shook my hand. "Steven Callister. No big deal."

It was the beginning of our friendship.

Steven was a freshman, too. It was his first year at Los Lunas High, and after that first day I stuck pretty close to him on campus.

One Friday, a couple of weeks after the bus incident, I invited him to go riding with me next day on the reservation.

He hesitated. "My dad says the reservation rangelands are off-limits to non-Indians."

"It's okay, long as you're with me."

"Sounds great," he agreed.

Saturday morning he showed up at my house on his black-and-white pinto mare, Tammy. I admired her sleek markings, then introduced Steven to my brown Appaloosa gelding, Sundance. He checked the spot patterns on Sundance's rump and gave an approving nod.

"C'mon," I said. "Got something to show you."

I led him to a walk-in cage near the chicken coops

11

behind our house. Inside the cage two young Cooper's hawks were perched on dead limbs that were propped in one corner. "They're not old enough to train yet, but they're gonna make fine hunters."

He studied the two birds. "Where'd you get them?"

"Black Mesa."

I explained how I took the birds from their nests as soon as they were old enough to survive on their own.

He noticed the fur on the floor. "Rabbits?"

"Uh-huh. They like live ones. I got traps set in the Manzanos. Wanta help me run them?"

"Sure."

That was the first of many happy days we spent riding the vast mountain rangelands of the reservation. And it was on such a day, the following February, that we came face-to-face with the killer bull.

There were many surprises in store for us that day. We set out early, riding north alongside the irrigation ditch. We were close pals by then and I felt at ease talking to Steven about most anything. Once, on an earlier ride, I asked him how he'd become tough enough to buck a guy like Bulldog Jenkins.

"My dad had to move around a lot," he said. "I was always the new kid in school. You know how that is."

I didn't, but I said, "Yeah."

At the large cottonwood grove the trees were still barren from winter. Bordering the grove, a high chain link fence marked the boundary between the reservation and private lands. On the other side of the fence, a dozen or more quarter horse colts were grazing on new alfalfa shoots. "That's the Rocking C Ranch," I said. "Mr. Cole's place."

"I know. My dad bought some mares from him."

"Someone else lives there, too, huh, Amigo? *Brenda* Cole."

12

"Who cares?" Steven snapped.

"Ha! Who cares? I see the way she wiggles by you at school, and rolls her big baby blues." I pantomimed with exaggerated gestures, twisting my body from side to side in the saddle and rolling my eyes skyward.

"Aw, chill out, okay?"

After a moment I said, "Bulldog's got the hots for Brenda too, you know. Has since seventh grade."

Steven didn't reply, but I saw his jaw tighten.

Near the middle of the grove there was a series of shallow pools where two irrigation ditches met and overflowed. They stank of surface algae so thick that no water could be seen. Near the pools, thickets of shoulder-high marsh grass, capped with fuzzy brown cattails, swayed in the breeze. Suddenly, from one of the thickets, a cock pheasant flushed and flew right across our path. Startled by the sudden drumbeat of wings, Tammy jerked backward, almost toppling Steven from the saddle. "Whoa! Whoa!" he commanded. It took a while to get her settled.

Unaffected by the disturbance, Sundance stood still.

"Good boy, Sundance." I patted his neck. "Pay no attention to frightened mares."

Steven flushed. "Man . . . they're gonna haul you off to the funny farm someday, talking to horses like that."

"No way, Amigo. That's the way of my people. My grandfather taught me."

"Your grandfather?"

"Pete Baca. Everybody knows about him . . . ask your dad. Grandpa was real famous once, probably the greatest *vaquero* in all history. Knows more about horses than anybody in the world. He always talked to horses. You better learn too if you want to become a real *vaquero*." I reached over and scratched his pinto

13

between the ears. "You understand me, don't you, Tammy? Scared little mare."

Tammy snorted.

"See, she knows," I said.

"Balls," Steven retorted.

A movement in the reeds caught my eye. I put a finger to my lips. "Shhhh."

At the far end of one pool, a fat muskrat waddled through the marsh grass and slithered into the water.

"Now, watch," I whispered.

All at once a V-shaped ripple appeared near where the muskrat had disturbed the water. At the point of the V an orange-brown fin broke through the algae. "Mud carp," I said. "Big ones, too. They get trapped in here every year." I dismounted. "Let's hog some of 'em."

"Hog?"

"Wade in. Grab 'em by the gills. Just don't grab a fin. Man, they sting."

"Far out!" He threw a leg over the saddle and jumped down and started to take off his boots.

"Leave 'em on," I said. "There're broken bottles and cans and all sorts of crap in there."

I unbuckled my spurs and threw them on the bank. Steven did the same. He wore the same type spurs that I wore. Unlike the cruel Spanish instruments that could rip a horse's flanks to shreds, our spurs were short, blunt stubs, meant only for prodding.

We waded in. Stagnant water poured over the tops of our boots. "Oh, Man!" Steven exclaimed. "Does this stuff ever stink!"

"Thrash around," I said. "Drive 'em to the far side."

We kicked and slapped the scummy water, watching for the tell-tale V. A fin broke the surface near Steven. He made a lunge for it, slipped, and fell face forward

14

into the pool. He sat up in the mud. Putrid algae matted his hair and dribbled down his face. His hat bobbed on the surface beside him.

"Oh-h-h-h . . ." I cried, laughing so hard my sides hurt, "are you . . . ever . . . a stinking mess. 'The Thing' . . . from outer space . . ."

"Oh, yeah?" Steven slapped the water hard, sending algae spraying at me. I saw it coming and took a quick sidestep. It was a mistake. Losing my balance, I fell backward into the pool. "Yeow . . . Ouch!" I reached beneath me and pulled out the angry carp I'd sat on. His spiked dorsal fin was extended in full fury. "*Madre de Dios*!" I rubbed my rear end with my free hand. "He got me right where the sun don't shine."

It was Steven's turn to laugh.

After I released the carp, Steven and I helped each other to our feet. On the bank we collapsed into the dry grass, and the cottonwoods resounded with our laughter.

While we let the sun dry us, I said, "Hey . . . Steven."

"Yeah?"

"You ever . . . done it?"

"Done what?"

"You know, man. . . . *It*."

"You mean, with a girl?"

"Yeah."

He hesitated. Then he said, "Naw."

"Me neither," I admitted.

After a moment I said, "Bulldog says he has."

"Oh, yeah." Steven's voice was steel. "Who with?"

I laughed. "Keep cool, Amigo. Not *her*. With Rosie Barnes, he says."

"Oh . . . no kiddin'?"

15

"Bulldog says Rosie puts out."

"That what he says?"

"Yeah. Wonder if it's true."

"Know what I think? I think Bulldog's full of it."

"Yeah," I said. "Maybe." But I wondered if what he said was true.

It was nearing mid-morning. I pushed my hat back, stood up and rebuckled my spurs. "It's warming up. We better get to the traps."

Beyond the cottonwoods, the trail ascended the mountains. A mile later, a thousand feet above the valley, we entered a vast rangeland of piñon, yucca, salt bush and sage. Across the river behind us, poised like giant sentinels on the horizon, were the five dormant volcanos that centuries before had spit out the dark lava ash that discolored the trail where we now rode. This was Black Mesa.

At the mouth of a dry arroyo I reined back. Just ahead, a lone piñon stood straight and tall, its conical shape resembling a plains Indian's wigwam. "There's 'Teepee'," I said.

We rode to the tree. The rudimentary trap of sticks and wire at its base was empty. The lettuce bait beside the trigger was undisturbed.

"Damn!" Steven exclaimed.

"C'mon," I said. "Let's check the others."

The trap beneath 'Fat Man' was also empty. But the traps at 'Old Woman' and 'Running Bear' held rabbits. Both were cottontails, which didn't surprise me. I'd never been able to entice the wilier jack rabbits into a trap.

I dropped the second cottontail into the gunnysack with the first. Steven re-baited the trap and set the trigger. When he rose he took off his denim jacket and

16

slammed it against the tree. Chunks of dried gunk from the carp pool fell from the jacket. "My clothes feel like cement."

"Mine too." I held my hat in front of my eyes and stood in my stirrups, looking for a familiar landmark. "C'mon, follow me."

Ten minutes later we reined up on the crest of an arroyo much deeper and wider than the others. Below, in the broad flat bed, a towering windmill churned away in the high-plains wind. At the foot of the windmill several mixed-breed cattle were drinking from a huge steel water tank. Others lay in the mud of the tank's shady side, which was growing ever smaller with the approaching noonday sun.

"Amigo," I said, "let's go swimming." I spurred toward the tank.

With a shout of approval, Steven followed.

We peeled stark naked, tossed all our clothes into the tank, then climbed in ourselves. The water was frigid, but after the initial shock we took to it like trout to a mountain pool. We washed the matted algae from our hair and bodies, then beat and churned our clothes until they, too, were clean. Then we paddled around hollering and ducking each other. Water splashed over the sides of the tank. The cattle ambled off in disgust.

After a while I gathered my clothes, climbed out of the tank and went to a nearby piñon. The wind raised goose bumps on my flesh. "Hang your stuff here," I called to Steven. "It'll dry fast. I got some jerky in my saddle bag." I went to Sundance.

Steven had just hung his clothes on the piñon when there was an unexpected disturbance in the branches. I glanced up in time to see a hawk tumble from its nest. Too young for sustained flight, it flapped across the ground in short desperate spurts, trying to escape.

17

I jumped into the saddle. "Quick! He's a prize one!"

"Hey, man," Steven shouted. "We got nothing on!"

"Who's to see? HI-A Y-E-EE-E!" I shouted and rode after the hawk which had already disappeared over the far crest of the arroyo.

Steven ran to Tammy. "HI-A Y-E-EE-E" I heard him yell behind me. Moments later he caught up with me. Side by side, whip-dried by the wind, we repeated the ancient war cry as we topped the crest at full gallop and raced down the far side.

I don't know which one of us saw her first, but there she was—just over the crest, mounted on her gray mare, Maude. She had pushed her hat to the back of her head and her red hair reflected the sun like burnished copper. She was wearing faded jeans, rawhide boots, and a snap-button shirt—just like any boy. But no one would ever mistake Brenda Cole for a boy.

Brenda stared incredulously as we two naked horsemen bore down on her shouting a blood-curdling yell.

"Oh, no!" I exclaimed, recognizing her.

"Oh, crap!" Steven cried. I knew he recognized her too.

We pulled our mounts back on their haunches and slid to a stop right in front of her, kicking up a cloud of dust and sand that pelted her from head to foot. Ignoring the dirt shower, Brenda flashed a mischievous smile. "Hi, guys. Where's the party?"

In one simultaneous movement Steven and I reined about and sped back over the crest.

"Hey . . . wait up!" Brenda yelled, and spurred Maude after us.

Mortified, Steven and I kicked our mounts and leaned low in the saddle, leaving our pursuer with an up close and personal view of two bare butts, one

18

cinnamon brown, the other pale pink, bouncing in the noonday sun.

"Aw, come on, Brenda," I begged, "throw us our pants, huh?"

We'd outraced her to the tank and dived in just as she caught up with us. Cowering up to our necks in water, we pleaded for our clothes. She stood beside the piñon, holding our pants out in front of her. "You guys chicken?" she taunted. "They're right here." Her ice-blue eyes sparkled at our discomfiture.

She kept up the cat and mouse game. We were animals at bay. We began to shiver. Then, all at once, Steven uttered an oath and stood straight up. "Screw this. I'm getting my clothes."

He climbed out of the tank and headed straight for Brenda. Eyes wide as saucers, she threw our pants back on the piñon and turned her back to him. "Okay...okay!" She gave a nervous chuckle. "Game's over."

"The hell it is." Steven grabbed her by the arm.

She squealed. Twisting from his grasp she ran to the other side of the piñon. "You keep away from me, Steven Callister, you hear? Don't you dare . . ."

With a loud guffaw, Steven grabbed his clothes from the tree and started putting them on. I climbed out of the tank and did the same.

We started back across the mesa together. Riding between us, Brenda was silent, her face contorted in a little-girl pout. Steven reined closer to her. "Hey, I don't see why you got your nose so out of joint. David and me're the ones oughta be pissed."

After a moment she looked up at him and her pretty smile returned. "You're right. Friends?"

"Friends," Steven said.

"Me, too," I added.

Cheerful now, we rehashed and laughed over the scene at the water tank as we rode back toward the valley.

Near 'Fat Man' I stopped. "Let's cut through the mud flats. It's tricky, but a lot faster."

We rode downhill to the river. In this section of the valley a heavy stand of Russian Olive trees stretched for miles along the east bank of the Rio Grande. Bush-like, growing to a height of twenty feet, they tended to clump together. At the edge of the trees the chalky clay soil, baked hard after last year's floods, was parched and deep lined. It reminded me of the faces of the old men who gathered each day on the porch of the pueblo community center to reminisce and swap yarns.

A vinegary-sweet aroma hung in the air. Steven sniffed. "What's that smell?"

"The trees are beginning to bud," I explained. "You guys be careful. They got thorns."

We entered the thicket, hunched low in our saddles to ward off drooping branches. Near the center of the flats the clay turned to mud, slowing us even more. "This is the worst," I said. "It'll thin out soon."

"Sooner the better," Brenda said.

A few yards further along, the trail widened and the trees grew wider apart. I sat up. "Well, we made . . ."

Just then Sundance gave a loud snort and balked. "Whoa, boy! Steady," I said, as he sidled off the trail.

"Ha!" Steven exclaimed. "Now whose horse is spooky?"

Sundance's nostrils flared and his eyes widened with fear. I ignored Steven's chiding. "You guys hold tight rein and follow me, close." I tried to hide my anxiety.

I forced Sundance's head about and urged him on. He moved with hesitant, reluctant steps. Then I saw

20

what I feared I might. Just ahead of us the trail was marked with deep, cloven hoof prints. They were freshly made by an enormous animal. Just then a bone-chilling bellow ruptured the stillness, followed by a low and angry rumble that rose threateningly, as if coming from the very bowels of the earth.

"Oh, God!" I cried. "Brenda! Steven! Get out of here, quick!" I spurred Sundance hard.

Brenda raced ahead. Steven was not in sight. I glanced back and saw him staring, transfixed, into the thicket. Less than twenty feet from him, a gargantuan brown-and-white splotched bull was ripping the ground with his hoof, throwing mud high over his massive back. His head was cocked to one side, and his eye—a single demonic eye—was fixed on Tammy's belly. Terrified, the pinto whinnied and lurched to one side, jerking the reins from Steven's hands.

I wheeled about and rode back. "Steven! Move! Spur on!"

The terror in my voice shocked him back to reality. He leaned far over Tammy's neck, grabbed the fallen reins and spurred the mare hard. "Go!" he shouted.

Side by side we plunged headlong through the trees, ignoring the thorny branches that whipped us from all sides. At the edge of the thicket we crossed hard clay and hit the irrigation ditch trail at a dead run. We didn't slow until we caught up with Brenda at the cottonwood grove, two miles further along.

The horses were coated with lather. I shifted in the saddle and looked back along the trail. It was clear. I signaled for a dismount. "Better rest the horses."

"Us too," Steven said.

We sat with our backs against an uprooted cottonwood. Brenda wet a bandana from her canteen and cleaned the scratches on our faces. "Nothing serious, guys," she assured us.

21

After a few minutes our breathing returned to normal.

"What *was* that thing?" Steven asked.

"That," I replied, "was Diablo."

"Hey!" Brenda exclaimed. "The devil steer!"

"You better believe it."

She gave an involuntary shiver. "My grandfather tells some scary tales about him."

Steven gave us a quizzical look. "Would one of you please tell me what the hell you're talking about?"

I leaned over and picked up a stick and drew a crude outline of a steer in the dirt. On the right side of his head I drew a curved horn, long and sharp. On the left side I drew a stub. "He's a *corriente*," I said. "A Mexican mixed breed, like the ones at the water tank. But different—a helluva lot different. My father says he's the biggest *corriente* anyone's ever seen."

"What do you mean, 'devil steer'?"

I sat back against the fallen trunk. "He's not a true steer. He's more like . . . well, a half-bull. All my people know about Diablo." I tossed the stick aside and told the story.

"Every spring our *vaqueros* ride to the mountains to round up strays. They always find new calves with the maverick cows. When a rider finds a male calf he cuts him, right there on the spot."

"Castrates him?" Steven asked.

"Yeah. But sometimes it's a bad cut. The calf becomes a steer that's not a true steer, but not a real bull either. He can still . . . well . . ."

Brenda came to my rescue. "Mount a heifer," she said.

"Yeah, that's right. But he can't make a calf. Some people call them 'stags'. That's what happened to Diablo. Nine . . . ten years ago, they found this male calf and his mother way back in the Manzanos. He'd been

22

clawed up real bad. His left eye had been ripped from its socket. They figured he'd been torn up by a puma. His mother probably ran the cat off before it could kill him. The *vaqueros* cut him right there, and that night mother and calf slipped away and went back to the mountains. Lots of mavericks live out their lives like that, running wild. Mostly they don't hurt nothing. But Diablo was different.''

"How?"

"He was meaner'n hell," I said. "About five years ago, the *vaqueros* started bringing back stories about a giant *corriente* steer they kept spotting up in the mountains. He was always with a bunch of heifers. The riders recognized the heifers as ones that had disappeared from stock pens on the Pueblo. The steer's body was scarred up real bad from fights with other bulls. And, he had only one horn.

"Three summers ago, Martino Silva came back from the mountain with his leg all banged up. He'd tie-fasted the big steer—roped him with the lariat tied to the saddle horn . . .''

"I know what tie-fast means," Steven said bluntly.

"Oh . . . sure. Anyway, the steer pulled Martino's horse over like he was a toy. Dragged them across the ground with Martino's leg pinned under the horse. Martino pulled his stock knife and cut the rope. He got his horse to his feet just as the steer turned and charged. Martino reined back hard, making the horse rear up. The horn missed the horse's gut, but it ripped his flank wide open. He came down running and Martino let him run, all the way back to the valley.

"That night everyone went to Martino's house to hear the story. He was propped up in a chair with lots of bandages on his leg. While he was on the ground he got a good look at the one-horned steer. The bull's left eye was gone. The other one, Martino said, stared

23

at him like a demon. '*Ojo de Diablo*,' Martino said—the eye of the devil. Then someone mentioned the scrawny one-eyed calf from the Manzanos years before and everyone knew it was him. From that night on they called him 'Diablo'—the devil steer.''

"No damned wonder," Steven said.

"You know, Amigos . . . we must have had a guardian angel riding with us back there." I crossed myself. "I just don't understand why Diablo didn't charge us. He's put a lot of *vaqueros* in the hospital."

"Why don't they shoot the bastard?" Steven asked.

"That's what my grandfather says," Brenda added. "But he says the pueblo council won't permit it."

"Yeah," I confirmed. "There've been a lot of arguments about it. But the council keeps siding with the younger *vaqueros*. It's like a game with them. They wanta drag Diablo into the plaza at the end of a rope. They know whoever does it will be a big man on the reservation. My father says it'll never happen."

"Why?" Steven asked.

"To hold a steer that big takes two ropers—a header and a heeler. My father says the problem is the header horse. There's not one big enough or strong enough to hold Diablo until the heeler gets a rope on his hind legs."

Story ended, we grew quiet. The sun had penetrated what little shade we had from the leafless trees. On the far side of the irrigation ditch, a prairie dog emerged from his hole, stood at attention for a full minute, then scampered off in search of frolic or food. I watched until he disappeared, then pulled my hat low over my eyes and leaned back to rest.

After a long silence Steven said, "I know a horse that could hold him."

"Huh?"

"I said, I know a horse that could hold the bastard, long enough for you to heel-rope him."

Brenda sat up with a start. "Cheyenne! Your dad's roping horse."

"You better believe it," Steven said.

I pushed my hat back and gave them both a hard look. "Did I hear you say, until *I* could heel-rope him?"

"That's what I said," Steven replied.

I leaned forward and searched his face for some sign that he wasn't serious. "You *are* joking, right? You don't really believe that you and me . . ."

He jumped to his feet and made a show of swinging a lariat. He was exhilarated. "Why not? Cheyenne's the strongest horse in New Mexico—in the whole world, I bet. And he's a trained roping horse. Look, you can handle a lariat. So can I. Think about it. Dragging that ornery bastard steer into the plaza—you and me!"

I looked at my friend as if I were seeing him for the first time. He was plumb loco. Still, what he said did have appeal. It *would* be something. Steven and me . . . dragging Diablo . . .

Crazy!

I forced my thoughts back to reality. "Look, Amigo,"—I shook my head—"it's not just the header horse. It's . . . well . . . it's us. We're not real *vaqueros*."

Steven started to say something else, but Brenda spoke first. "David's right, Steven."

His face showed real disappointment. He sat back against the tree. After a while he said, "Yeah, I guess so."

One month later Tino Valdez and Manuel Tome brought my father home in a pick-up truck, his leg

25

torn open. As I stood at the foot of my father's bed that Saturday morning of my fifteenth birthday, I recalled that earlier day with my friends on the mesa: the water tank, the Russian Olive tree thicket, Steven's narrow escape. Most of all I remembered Steven's eagerness to go after Diablo. I'd argued against it then. Now, things had changed. It was time for me to become a real *vaquero*.

With a silent vow to my sleeping father, I left to ride to the Callister ranch, to tell my friend that at last I was ready to even the score with the devil steer.

Chapter 3

The next morning, after mass, I saddled Sundance and rode to the cottonwood grove. After a while, far down the dirt trail, a rider appeared. I stood in the stirrups and waved. "Steven . . . Yo!"

When he reined up beside me I stared in awe. I'd never seen him before on any mount other than Tammy. Because she was smaller than Sundance, Steven and I were always eye-to-eye in the saddle. Now, mounted on Cheyenne, he loomed over me like a hawk over a sparrow.

"Man . . . he's *big*!" I exclaimed.

Over seventeen hands at the withers, with a broad muscular back and powerful haunches, the giant silver-maned palomino was as famous among horsemen and rodeo buffs as was his owner.

"Your dad say it's okay?" I asked.

"To ride him. I didn't tell him what for."

We had agreed, in the corral behind Steven's home yesterday when I told him what Diablo had done to my father. Steven had struck his palm with his fist. "That does it. Let's go after him."

"I shoulda listened to you before. Can you get Cheyenne tomorrow?"

He didn't give it a second thought. "I'll get him. What's the plan?"

Like collaborating war chiefs we knelt and drew tactical diagrams in the dirt. With the stronger horse, Steven would be the header. His job would be to rope Diablo's head and hold him tight until I could come up from the rear and rope his hind legs. "You'll have to wear him down first," I said. "I'm not the best heeler in the world."

"No sweat," Steven said.

"He's only got one eye. He always puts his head down like this and paws the ground just before he charges." I cocked my head and pawed dirt. "Try to get a rope on him before that. One last thing—if you do rope him and he starts to drag you . . . even an inch . . . cut rope and spur out of there fast. Bring your knife, hear?"

"Sure. Don't sweat it. Cheyenne'll know how to handle him."

I believed that was true—if the palomino was strong enough. I kept my doubts to myself. "Okay, Amigo. *Mañana*, at the cottonwoods."

"*Mañana*, at the cottonwoods," he repeated, and we did a high five on it.

It was from the cottonwood grove that Sunday morning that we set off on our quest for the devil steer. Two miles from the grove, we came to the embankment where Steven, Brenda and I had raced out of the mud flats at a dead run the month before. Near here, yesterday, my father had been gored. Today, there was a light breeze to our backs. "We're upwind," I complained. "He might catch our scent before Sundance catches his."

The Appaloosa was calm.

"If he's in there," Steven said.

"He's in there. I can feel it."

We rode down the bank and entered the thicket, pacing the horses at a slow gait, alert for any unusual sight or sound. Fifteen minutes later we broke out onto open range. I reined to a stop. "He won't be out here."

"How about the mountains?" Steven suggested.

"Too much territory. Let's ride south, drag the flats from the lower end. Maybe—"

Just then Sundance gave a nervous snort and flared his nostrils. "Look alive!" I cried.

Sundance whinnied and sidled, shying away from the thicket. I glanced around. "It's got to be him! But where? I don't see—"

"There!" Steven stood in the stirrups and pointed. "In that clump of trees!"

I spotted him. Fifty yards away, half-hidden among the trees, Diablo stood watching our every move. With an angry toss of his head, the huge brown-and-white *corriente* bull lumbered out onto the mesa like an army tank geared for combat.

"*Dios*! Look at the size of him!" I glanced all around. "We're too close to the thicket. C'mon."

We raced uphill until we were well onto open range, then stopped and wheeled about. Diablo followed.

"He's gonna do it," I said. "He's gonna take us on."

Our eyes were riveted on the approaching steer. Two hundred feet away, Diablo stopped, raised his head and flared his nostrils as if to confirm a hated scent. Then the massive head lowered and cocked to one side. The single rapier horn jutted out, only inches above the ground. With an savage snort, he began to paw the ground, throwing dirt across his broad back and high into the air.

Like a sudden blow to the belly, reality struck me. *This wasn't make-believe.* In about twenty seconds, two-thousand pounds of enraged bull would charge at

29

us like a runaway freight train. My heart pounded like a triphammer, rocking me in the saddle. I couldn't remove my gaze from that deadly horn. Trying to keep my voice under control I said, "Look, Amigo . . . you sure you wanta do this . . . it's not too la—"

A wild cry cut me short: "HI-AY-E-EE-E!" With that defiant challenge Steven raised his lariat high and spurred Cheyenne into a headlong charge straight at Diablo.

With mighty strides, the palomino closed the gap. Diablo stood his ground, horn poised for the grisly plunge into Cheyenne's soft underbelly. Ten feet from his quarry, Steven pressed his right knee against Cheyenne's side. At the silent command the stallion veered left and Steven threw the rope. It was too high. But as horse and rider sped by, Diablo, caught off guard by the unexpected maneuver, raised his head to keep them in sight. The tip of his horn caught the flared loop. At the touch of the rope he tossed his head. Too late. The loop settled down around the base of his good horn and across the stump of the deformed one. The rope snapped taut, yanking Diablo's head to the right. Sensing the noose set, Cheyenne dug in and backed, allowing no slack to form in the rope.

"I got him! I got him!" Steven yelled. Anticipating the struggle to come, he grabbed the saddle horn where the lariat was tied and held on.

"Watch him!" I yelled. "He's tricky!"

Lariat in hand I circled in a wide arc to approach Diablo from behind.

The bull thrashed his head from side to side, but it only tightened the noose that held him fast. Changing tactics, he lunged forward, causing the rope to slacken momentarily. Just as quickly, Cheyenne backed to take up the slack. But, again Diablo lunged forward, and again Cheyenne countered, turning to one side or the

30

other at just the right moment to keep the rope tight. Diablo began to circle. Like the hub of a wheel Cheyenne pivoted slowly, keeping his head toward the bull, sensing and countering Diablo's every move. With each maneuver I saw for myself why the golden stallion had won all honors as World Champion Roping Horse.

Again and again I tried to get close enough to Diablo's rear to rope one or both of his hind feet. Each time, his erratic movements prevented it. Signaling my frustration to Steven I withdrew to one side. He understood. There was nothing I could do until Diablo tired.

It was noon. Overhead, the blazing sun beat down without mercy. You don't sweat often in desert country. But, even from my distance, I could see the rivers of perspiration that rolled down Steven's face, causing him to shake his head often to clear his eyes. Oblivious to all—scorching sun, choking dust, blinding sweat—the palomino stallion and the *corriente* bull pitted brute strength against brute strength, countering each other in a duel for survival.

A half-hour into the fight, Diablo lowered his head and ceased his struggles, as if exhausted. Suddenly, he lunged forward a couple of yards. Then he reversed direction and threw his whole weight into a mighty backward tug against the rope. Caught off guard, Cheyenne stumbled and fell to his knees.

My heart skipped beats. Cheyenne was being dragged! "Steven!" I yelled. "Cut rope . . . cut rope!"

The big stallion struggled to his feet. Muscles bulging, he dug his hooves into the dirt, locked his forelegs and leaned far back on his haunches, his rump almost on the ground. The dragging ceased. Frustrated, Diablo repeated the tactic, lunging forward then immediately reversing direction. This time it didn't work.

31

Cheyenne was anchored like granite. Diablo couldn't budge him.

"He's holding!" Steven shouted. "I told you! He's holding!"

"*Ole!*" I grabbed my lariat. "Back him, Amigo. Hard."

Steven grabbed the reins and pulled back. Straining every muscle in his body, Cheyenne began to move backward, slowly, inch by agonizing inch. Diablo dug his hooves into the dirt and shook his head fiercely. It was in vain. He was being dragged! For the first time in his life the proud bull had met a superior force.

"Way to go, Amigo! Way to go." I twirled my lariat. With each involuntary lurch forward Diablo lifted his rear hooves high. It was an easy target now, even for me. I closed in from the rear.

There was a sudden loud 'Snap!'

Diablo stumbled backward. When he rose, the loop end of Steven's lariat dangled from his head, frayed at the end where it had broken under the strain. At the instant of the break, the other section of the rope, tied fast to Steven's saddle horn, lashed back through the air and struck Cheyenne's nose, slicing like a cat-o'-nine-tails into the soft flesh. Startled, the palomino emitted a loud whinny and reared. High . . . Higher . . .

For breathless moments, like a park statue rooted in time, rider and horse froze in that upright position. Then, losing balance, Cheyenne fell over backward, slamming Steven to the ground. The full weight of the giant horse came crashing down upon my friend.

Cheyenne scrambled to his feet. Riderless now, maddened with pain, he bolted across the mesa. On the ground, Steven pushed up on one elbow and tried to sit up. "DAV-V-V-V . . . !" he screamed, then fell back, silent.

I reined up hard and jumped from the saddle before

Sundance could stop. Steven lay still. His right leg was twisted beneath him and his eyes were closed. A fist-size swelling discolored his face. Beneath his twisted leg the ground was turning red with blood.

I dropped on the ground beside him. "Oh, God . . . Oh, God!" I grasped his wrist and tried to find a pulse, but couldn't. "Oh, God . . . Steven!" I lifted his head into my lap and began to weep. In that agonizing moment I could think of only one thing. "Steven . . . are you baptized?" I licked my thumb and placed it in the center of his forehead. Then, blinded by tears, I made the sign of the cross. "In the . . . name of the Father . . . and . . . and of the Son . . . and of . . ."

From behind me came the ominous sound of a hoof pawing the ground. I whirled around, and my blood turned ice-cold. Less than fifty feet away, Diablo was tearing at the earth in rage. His head was lowered. This time the rapier horn was pointed right at me.

Sundance was nowhere in sight. In desperation, I looked toward the thicket. A hundred yards. My only chance. I jumped up and grasped Steven under the arms and tried to lift him, but he was dead weight. Diablo began his charge. Terror-stricken, holding my unconscious friend half-way off the ground, I stood rooted in place and stared into the face of approaching death.

An instant later, the unmistakable 'Crack!' of rifle fire resounded across the mesa and Diablo toppled headlong onto the ground. He lay for a moment in shock, then struggled to his feet. Just below his left shoulder a tiny red splotch appeared, then spread. With a wild beast's instinct for survival, he turned away from the direction from which the pain had come, fled toward the flats and disappeared into the thicket.

Someone was shaking my shoulder. "David. Put him down."

The voice was hollow, dreamlike, familiar.

"David!"

I forced my eyes from where Diablo had disappeared into the thicket and looked up into the face of Tino Valdez.

"Let me have him, David."

Tino took Steven from me and lowered him back onto the ground. For the first time I noticed that I was trembling. I couldn't control it. "How . . . how did you . . . ?" Chalk-dry, my mouth wouldn't work right, the words wouldn't come.

"I came to see what was causing all the dust. Take deep breaths, David." Tino knelt and felt the arteries on Steven's neck.

"Tino . . . is he . . . ?"

"No. Not yet."

He ran his hand over Steven's misshapen leg, stopping at the thigh. "The bone's sticking out. That's where the blood's coming from."

He reached into his pocket and withdrew his stockman's knife and cut Steven's jeans from cuff to hip. Just above Steven's right knee a jagged bone protruded through torn flesh. I gagged.

"David! Get control!" Tino looked closer at the wound. "Blood's congealing. Good." He turned his attention to Steven's head. The right side of his face was swollen and deep purple, the left side chalk-white. Tino stuck his hand inside Steven's shirt. "Clammy."

Tino rose and went to his horse. He unstrapped a blanket from behind the saddle then took his Winchester rifle from its scabbard. He came back and put the blanket over Steven, tucking it up around his neck.

I still hadn't moved. I just stood there, looking down at my stricken friend, tears streaking the dirt on my face. Tino put a hand on my shoulder. "David, you've got to ride. Understand?"

I wiped my eyes on my sleeve and nodded.

"Take my horse. Manuel is putting out salt blocks near the water tank. He's got the pick-up. Tell him to come fast."

I turned to go.

"Wait," Tino said. He checked the rifle to make sure there was a live round in the chamber, then sat down facing the Russian Olive trees. "After you find Manuel, ride to the boy's home. Tell his parents we're taking him to Saint Anne's. Now, go fast."

I mounted Tino's horse and spurred hard for the water tank.

Chapter 4

One item in that overheated waiting room remains seared into my memory: the large Seth Thomas clock mounted above the double doors leading to surgery. Far into the night I stared at that octagonal clock with its black stiletto hands and outmoded Roman numerals. But my thoughts were not on time. Again and again, in my mind I relived the horror that had brought me to this place: the giant palomino crashing down on Steven; my helplessness in the face of Diablo's charge; Tino's life-saving rifle shot; my frantic ride to the Callister home; Mr. Callister's questioning look as I rode up alone, his face changing to an alabaster mask as I related my grim news; my gallop back toward Route 47 to rendezvous with Manuel Tome's truck with Steven lying in the bed, unconscious and ghostly pale. It came to me, as I sat in that speeding truck watching Tino cradle Steven's shattered leg to keep the bone from puncturing an artery, that this was the second time in twenty-four hours that these men, in this truck, had been pitted in a race against time with a victim of Diablo.

Forty minutes from the time he helped load Steven into the truck bed, Manuel pulled to a stop at the ambulance entrance of Saint Anne's Hospital in Albuquerque. Steven's parents were already there. Gripping hands, Mr. and Mrs. Callister followed the gurney bearing their son to the emergency room. When I started to follow, too, Tino put an arm on my shoulder. "Better come back with us, David."

I shook my head. "I'm staying."

He looked at me for a moment, then nodded. "I'll explain to your mother." He left with Manuel to return to the reservation.

There were a half-dozen people, maybe more, seated in the blue molded-plastic chairs in the waiting room outside surgery. Some leafed through old magazines, carried on muted conversations, or watched a wall-mounted TV. A couple of them simply stared at the floor. One or two glanced up when I entered. I took one of the chairs nearest the surgery doors, held my hat in my lap, and vowed to remain there until I knew about Steven, no matter how long I had to wait.

Once, during the early hours of that long evening, I overheard bits and pieces of a discussion between a doctor and a nurse who emerged from behind the double doors. They were talking about the boy who had been "crushed by a horse." I recognized some of their muted words: "concussion," "compound fracture," "blood loss," "critical." Despite the others in the room, I felt very much alone.

Much later, I became aware that the waning daylight filtering through the waiting-room skylight had at last given way to darkness. I looked at the Seth Thomas. Twenty minutes past eight. Eight hours since the accident; seven since we'd gotten to the hospital. From time to time during those somber hours, Steven's father would emerge from somewhere beyond those foreboding double doors, get two cups of coffee from a coin-operated dispenser down the hall, then go back to wherever he and Mrs. Callister were waiting. If he knew I was there he made no sign of it. I thought about that. To my father, Steven was always "that gringo boy." I wondered if to Jess Callister I was "that Indian boy."

Sometime after nine o'clock, Steven's mother came through the double doors and walked up to where I was sitting. I was still smelly and dirty, just like I had come off the mesa earlier. Mrs. Callister's name was Milli and she was a real pretty dark-haired lady. In the few times I'd been to her home, she'd always treated me nice. Now her face was creased with strain. I wondered if she was going to put the blame on me. No matter what she said, she couldn't make me feel any worse. To my surprise she reached down and took my hand. "Come, David."

She led me through the double doors and down a corridor to a place marked CRITICAL CARE UNIT. She held back the curtains of one cubicle so I could enter. Steven lay flat on his back in a high bed. His head was swathed in bandages. Only his discolored right eye remained uncovered, and it was swollen closed. His right leg, encased in a plaster cast from hip to ankle, was suspended high on a wire bolted to a frame in the ceiling. At the cast, the wire was attached to both ends of a steel pin inserted just below his knee. Some sort of clear liquid dripped from a plastic bag through a tube to a needle inserted in Steven's left arm. The arm was strapped to a board.

Mr. Callister was standing at the head of the bed. He glanced at me then looked away.

Mrs. Callister said, "He's sedated."

The words stung. Only yesterday, beside another bed, my mother had uttered the same words about my father. And for the same reason—Diablo.

Mrs. Callister continued: "His leg was crushed. He's going to be here for a long time, then be bedridden for several weeks after he gets home. Those are going to be hard days for him, David. Hard . . . lonely days." She put her hand on my shoulder. "He's going to need a friend now more than ever."

There was no blame in her voice. I looked up at her. Her eyes were on Steven, had been all the time she was talking to me I guessed. I said, "He won't be lonely . . . I promise."

It was the only time during those dreadful hours that I saw her smile. She gave my shoulder a squeeze.

Silently, I repeated the vow to myself. I would spend every moment I could with my friend.

But first, unknown to me then, there was another crisis already in the making that was coming down, straight at me.

Chapter 5

It came in the form of Brenda Cole.

She was Chad Cole's granddaughter. That alone meant that she was destined to grow up in a world devoted to horses. When she was only six days old her grandfather had cradled her in his arms, mounted his favorite quarter horse stallion, and cantered twice around the hacienda corral, one of seventeen working corrals on Mr. Chad's sixty-five thousand acre Rocking C Ranch. From that day on, Brenda was hooked. For her fourth birthday, Mr. Chad had presented her with a gentle, dapple-gray mare that was foaled the same day Brenda was born. She'd named the mare 'Maude'. Ever since that day, flame-haired Brenda Cole and dapple-gray Maude had claimed the trails and mesas of the lower Rio Grande Valley as their own, including the reservation.

None of my people protested. For over fifty years any of us down on his luck had been able to find a job on the Rocking C, and been paid wages according to his work, not according to his color. For this reason, the pueblo boundary signs that proclaimed "ISLETA INDIAN RESERVATION—NO TRESPASSING!" were recognized by the pueblo police patrols to contain an unwritten footnote: *Except for Señor Chad Cole's granddaughter*.

It was the Saturday morning, a week after Steven's accident, that my mother called out to the corral where I was currying Sundance and said I was wanted on the phone. "Brenda Cole," she said when I got to the house. She smiled. My mother thought I was stuck on Brenda. Fact was, every boy in the valley was stuck on Brenda.

When I answered 'Hi', Brenda said without preliminaries, "David, I want to talk to you. Where can we meet?"

It wasn't the most pleasant tone I'd ever heard her use. If she'd wanted to chat about Steven, like before, we'd have done it on the phone. I got a sinking feeling in my stomach. This was about something else, and I had a sneaking suspicion I knew what.

"Saint Augustine?" I suggested. "Say, an hour?"

"See you there." Click!

The rutted dirt road from my home to the pueblo square led past timeworn adobe houses that had been occupied by my people for over six hundred years. Along the way, this morning the aroma of baking bread wafted from the blackened dome-shaped ovens that dotted the barren yards. From time to time, shawl-draped old women would look up from tending the ovens to watch me ride by. Now and then, a mangy dog would dart out to yap at Sundance's heels. As always, he ignored such irritations with a fine dignity.

Three-centuries-old, Saint Augustine Mission Church, with its massive external buttresses and ancient beamed ceiling, is the largest structure on Isleta Reservation. Like an adobe cathedral, it dominates the north side of the Pueblo's central plaza. This morning a score of tourists, just disembarked from a Green Line Tour Bus from Albuquerque, were snapping photos or

41

shopping for trinkets and baked goods at the pueblo store. Across the plaza, two pickups emblazoned with the seal of the tribal police were parked in front of the pueblo police headquarters. There were no horses in sight. I dismounted, tossed Sundance's reins over the hitching post outside the church courtyard and went through the wooden double doors into the old building. It took a moment for my eyes to adjust to the subdued light. At the far end of the cavernous sanctuary a lone woman was lighting a candle at the foot of a life-size crucifix. I dropped to one knee and crossed myself and started to take a seat on the first bench when a hushed voice called, "David . . . over here."

Brenda was seated next to the wall in a pew on the other side of the aisle. Her head was covered with a kerchief. I entered the pew and sat beside her. "I didn't see Maude outside."

"I walked," she replied.

It wasn't too far, but I was surprised.

"Thanks for coming, David."

"No problem." I glanced around the shadowy interior of the old church. As always, the aroma of burning wicks and melted wax hung in the air. "This is one of my favorite places. There're a lot of my ancestors here, you know."

"I know."

I scuffed a boot across the heavy pine boards. "There wasn't any wood floor back then, just dirt. When a person died they wrapped him in his blanket and buried him here. Then they did a ceremonial dance over the grave to pack it down."

"I know."

"With a priest and everything . . . Right here, years before the Mayflower landed back east . . . Father Ortega says there're hundreds buried here . . . maybe thousands."

42

"Probably."

"Steven and I sneaked in here one night. Through a window . . . That one, over there. Just us two, spent the whole night, alone with these dead spirits 'n all. Guys on the reservation been doing that since my grandfather was a boy. It was real spooky, I tell you . . . we didn't sleep none that night."

"Steven told me about it."

I was stalling and she knew it. She hadn't asked me here to talk about the history of Saint Augustine, or how guys on the reservation tested their manhood. Finally, I asked, "You been to the hospital?"

"Yesterday. He says he's got an infection in his leg now. He looks awful."

"He looks a helluva lot better'n he did."

"He says you come to see him every day."

"Yeah. They're bringing him home as soon as the infection clears up."

"I know. David . . . is it true you've got his horse?"

This was it. The reason she'd called, had asked me to meet her. I knew she didn't mean did *I* have Cheyenne, myself. She meant my people.

"Yes," I replied, without looking at her.

"When are you going to give him back?"

Silence.

"David, answer me," she demanded.

"How'd you find out?"

"My grandfather knows everything that happens on the reservation. Now quit acting dumb and answer my question. When are you going to give Cheyenne back?"

There was no good way to answer that question. "It's . . . well . . . there's this stupid thing about stock abandoned on the reservation . . . whoever finds it can claim . . . Aw, Brenda!" I leaned forward in the pew and shook my head in frustration. "It's Martino Silva.

43

He was riding fences in Burnt Tree Canyon, high up in the Manzanos. He stopped in a ponderosa grove to eat his lunch and he thought he saw a deer at the water hole there. He almost shot it. Had a bead on it and everything. Then he saw it was a horse, still saddled—the palomino. He roped him and brought him down. A lot of us think he should give the horse back. But Martino's stubborn. He says he's got the right to claim Cheyenne as abandoned stock. The stock council's holding a special meeting about it tomorrow.''

"At the tribal office?''

"No. My, uh, father's on the council. He can't get up yet. They're meeting at our house.''

"David''—her voice was like ice—"Cheyenne belongs to Steven's dad!''

I didn't answer.

"David Baca. Are you Steven's friend or not?''

"Aw . . . c'mon, Brenda,'' I protested. "That ain't fair and you know it.''

"It's not fair to steal Mr. Callister's horse either.''

"Hey . . . it wasn't me!''

The woman in prayer at the altar looked around and frowned, so I lowered my voice. "Don't you think I'd like to do something, Brenda? I haven't even been able to sleep since I found out what was going on. But I'm just a kid, like you. I got no say-so with the council. None at all.''

She was on her feet before I could finish. "Don't hand me that 'just a kid' crap, David Baca. You weren't 'just a kid' when you took your best friend out on the mesa chasing after a wild bull. You better think of something fast, you hear me? Else you're not going to have a friend left in this valley, kid or otherwise.''

She stalked out before I could respond.

I slumped back on the bench in a blue funk. Brenda

was right. Unless I did something, or at least *tried*, to get Steven's horse back, my name would be mud. Mounted on the whitewashed plaster wall just above my head was a painting I'd known since childhood: the Virgin of Guadalupe. Gazing up into that familiar face I prayed aloud: "Santa Maria, help me, now."

Late that night, unable to sleep, I kicked off the covers, went to the living room and switched on MTV. Michael Jackson. It didn't help. I turned off the TV and just sat there in the dark, trying to sort it all out. I didn't hear my mother until she set a cup of cocoa on the end table beside me. She pulled her robe tighter around herself and sat down in a nearby chair. "You're troubled tonight."

I nodded and picked up the cup. The cocoa was hot and sweet. It tasted good.

"The horse?"

I slammed the cup down too hard, sloshing cocoa on the table. "Mama, it's not fair!"

"I know." She got up and went to the kitchen and came back with a towel to wipe the table.

When she sat back down I told her about the meeting with Brenda. All of it. She listened without interruption, letting me pour out the burden.

"She's right, too," I said. "Everybody's gonna come down on my case about this. I don't care about that. But I do care about Steven. I'm going to lose the best friend I ever had."

She placed her hand on mine. "You have no voice in these matters, I'm afraid. No one may speak before the council without invitation."

She hesitated, staring into a middle distance.

"Mama?"

No answer.

"Mama . . . What?"

45

She stood. "Let's go to bed, David."

"But, Mama . . ."

"Things will be all right. Try not to worry." She gave my hand a final pat and left.

I went to bed.

I worried.

Chapter 6

Next morning, my cup and bowl were set at my father's place. My mother was busy at the stove. Though we never spoke of it, she knew how proud I was to sit at the head of the table. I sat down and nodded to my grandfather, seated at the other end of the table. "Morning, Grandpa."

Grandpa Baca was ninety-two. He'd been over fifty when my father was born, ancient by the time I came along. Stooped and grizzled by time and the elements, he wore his long white hair in a single tight plat down his back. A patchwork of stains on the front of his robe revealed what he'd eaten for the past two days. At my greeting he muttered "Um, hmm," without looking up, and continued to blow on the coffee he'd just poured into his saucer. Mama's radio wasn't on, and I knew it was because Grandpa didn't like it. It was a concession she made only to him.

I took a cinnamon roll from a platter on the table and dipped it into my oatmeal. "I'm not going to school today."

"I know," my mother said. Then, with a sly wink, she whispered, "The meeting's at nine. There's a low window in that room."

I smiled at the suggestion.

47

After breakfast, I checked the fires in the ovens. Miguel had done well. I went to the barn and threw down some hay for Sundance, then sat on the hitching post by the tack room and waited.

The first pickup arrived at eight forty-five. Others arrived at intervals over the next fifteen minutes. At nine o'clock sharp, the chairman of the stock council, Sylvan Lujan, parked his Ford pickup in the yard, grabbed his gray plastic briefcase and went inside. I climbed over the corral fence and hurried to the other side of the house. There was a large window near the bed in my parent's room, its sill within three feet of the ground. The window was raised part way and a portable screen had been inserted to hold it up. I knew my mother had done that for me. I dropped to one knee and peeked through a corner of the screen. My father, wrapped in a blue terry-cloth robe, sat propped up in bed with his bandaged leg resting on a pillow. One by one the council members and witnesses entered the room, greeted my father, then took their places in the wooden folding chairs my mother and I had borrowed from Saint Augustine Church for this meeting.

Sylvan Lujan was last to enter. Short and bullet-shaped, with his countenance frozen in a perpetual frown, Chairman Lujan was not a man to be taken lightly. He pulled back the one chair at the table in the center of the room and sat down. He glanced toward my father. "Your leg's better, Ramon?" he asked, gruffly.

"Some," my father replied.

"Hmmm. Let's get started." Chairman Lujan ordered the door closed, announced that the stock council was officially in session, then nodded without comment to Martino Silva, seated against the wall near the door.

Martino stood and said, "My name is Martino

48

Silva." It was just a formality. Everyone in the room knew the finest and most popular of the Pueblo's young *vaqueros*. In a confident voice, Martino related in detail how he had found the golden horse while mending fences in Burnt Tree Canyon.

"He was abandoned stock?" Chairman Lujan asked.

"He was."

"There was no rider in sight?"

"None."

"He's now in your possession?"

"In my corral. I've taken good care of him."

"I'm sure. And now you claim ownership of this abandoned stock."

"I do."

There were murmurs of assent, and a nodding of heads around the room. I felt sick to my stomach.

Chairman Lujan slapped the table for silence. "Martino Silva, do you have a witness to support your claim?"

"Yes, Señor Lujan . . . Andy, here."

Seated next to Martino, an older, thickset man withdrew a red bandana, spit a wad of tobacco into it, then shoved the bandana back into his pocket. He rose on horseshoe-bowed legs. "Name's Andy Chavez," he said in a sluggish drawl.

Some of the council members chuckled. Andy Chavez had spent his younger years working in the uranium mines around Gallup. It was a standing joke on the reservation that he talked more like a white man than any Indian, give or take a Navajo or two.

In his own fashion, Andy confirmed Martino's story. " 'Course, now . . . I didn't right out *see* Martino catch 'im. But I seen him ride outa them ponderosas with 'im on a rope. Wasn't no one else up there, so that's same as seein' it. Wasn't no one gonna

49

give Martino a horse like that, now was they?''

More chuckling.

Never one for levity, Chairman Lujan rapped the table for silence. "You finished, Andy?''

"Reckon I am,'' Andy said, and sat down.

Chairman Lujan reached into his briefcase and withdrew Martino's petition. Then, clicking open his ballpoint pen he declared in an authoritative voice, "I see no need for further testimony. I'm sure the members of the council agree with me that Martino's petition should be approv—''

There was a loud knock.

Chairman Lujan shot a stern look toward the door. A meeting of the stock council was inviolable and no one, not even the pueblo governor, had authority to intervene. Chairman Lujan pushed back in his chair and splayed his hands flat on the table. Thus poised to do battle he ordered: "Open that door!''

Martino Silva obeyed the command.

At once, every man in the room except my bedridden father rose to his feet. Those wearing hats yanked them from their heads. Through the screen, I stared in disbelief. *Grandpa!*

Gone were the stained robe and worn corduroy slippers he'd had on at breakfast. In their place he wore a pair of whipcord trousers over black leather boots. His faded shirt had been replaced with one of white brocade with pearl snap-buttons. He leaned forward on his cane and surveyed the standing men through age-dimmed eyes.

Chairman Lujan sputtered, "*Señor . . . Señor . . .*'' fumbling for words.

I knew the reason. The chairman and council members were in the presence of a living legend: A man whose feats of horsemanship during his prime had brought fame to himself and his people. The silver-

50

crested cane in Grandpa's hand had once belonged to one of his most ardent admirers, Theodore Roosevelt. It had been presented to him by the old Rough Rider himself. Yet, few of the men gathered here today had ever seen Pete Baca this close. For two decades he had been a recluse in this house he had built with his own hands, over sixty years before.

"*Señors*," Grandpa said in a voice resonant with age, "I request the honor of addressing the council." He spoke with the precise English of one who had learned it in school as a second language.

Finding his voice at last, Chairman Lujan straightened to his full height. "Sir, the honor is ours. Martino! A chair for Señor Baca."

Grandpa shook his head. "I will stand."

"*Señor*," the chairman said, "if *you* stand, we *all* stand."

Grandpa glanced around the room. "Then I will sit."

Martino Silva placed his chair at Grandpa's side and helped the old man into it. Only then did the others return to their seats. Martino remained standing, leaning against the wall.

Grandpa asked, "This meeting is to discuss the golden horse?"

"Yes, *señor*," Chairman Lujan replied. "Martino Silva's rightful petition for ownership."

"Who among you speaks for Martino?" Grandpa asked.

"Martino speaks for himself, *señor*," Chairman Lujan explained. "He has made his statement—he has a witness . . ."

"Me!" Andy Chavez pointed out with pride.

Chairman Lujan cast Andy a fierce look.

Grandpa nodded. "And who among you speaks for Señor Callister?"

Silence.

"No one speaks for the Anglo?" Grandpa asked.

More silence.

"Then I will speak for him," Grandpa said.

Chairman Lujan coughed.

Some of the board members shifted in their seats.

"I am of the past," Grandpa said, straining to speak so all could hear. "Twice older then most in this room . . . three times some. In my lifetime I have seen many of our ways disappear. Some of the ways were good, and I was sad to see them disappear. Some were bad, and I was happy to see them disappear. Some of our ways are bad, and remain. One that is bad is the way that says a man's stock is no longer his stock if it strays onto our lands."

"Señor Baca," Chairman Lujan said, "that's not always true. Each case is considered . . ."

Ignoring the interruption, Grandpa said sharply, "Renaldo!"

In a chair near the window one middle-aged man, surprised to hear his name, sat forward. "*Señor?*"

"When you were a boy, Renaldo, your father would send you to the Anglo store for his tobacco, do you remember?"

"To Bosque Farms . . . for Bull Durham. Many times."

"And you rode your roan gelding . . . Apache."

"Ah, you remember his name. Yes."

"And one day you came out of the Anglo store to find that Apache had slipped his bridle and was gone."

"Why . . . that's the truth. I walked home that day. Eight miles. My father was very angry. He told me that now I'd have to walk always . . . I had no horse."

"And you walked always?"

Renaldo hesitated.

"And you walked always?" Grandpa persisted.

52

"No, *señor*. The next day Mr. Zolman came to my home. He brought Apache in his truck."

"Mr. Linn Zolman, the Anglo rancher?"

"That man . . . yes."

"He found Apache loose on his ranch and returned him to you."

"Yes, that's the truth."

Grandpa let the silence grow.

Chairman Lujan pulled a blue bandana from his hip pocket and wiped his brow. Some of the board members mumbled.

Ear pressed to the screen, I hung on every word.

Grandpa said, "Ramon!"

My father sat up straighter in bed. "Father?"

"When you were a child, Ramon, did you not own two black heifers?"

"Yes, you gave them to me."

"You were raising them to sell?"

"To make money to buy a saddle. . . . Yes."

"And you sold them and bought a saddle?"

"No. They broke out of the pen . . . they waded the river and got mixed in with the Rocking C herd. Mr. Cole's riders branded them."

"So, you lost your heifers, and your saddle?"

My father shook his head. "No. When Mr. Cole learned what had happened, he bought me a saddle . . . a Red River, with a solid oak roping tree." His voice turned wistful. "That was twenty-nine . . . no, thirty years ago. It's still a good saddle."

More silence.

After awhile Grandpa said, "Now, let us speak of the golden horse." All eyes were fixed on him.

"*Señors*, our ancient way with claiming strays was never meant for stock whose ownership could be proven. But even if it were, the golden horse did not *stray* onto our lands. The Anglo boy was not a trespasser. He was a guest of one of us . . . of my own grandson. If you decide in favor of Martino Silva—and I admire Martino Silva—you could destroy that friendship. Some, who live for yesterday, will say, 'That is of no consequence.' But I say, 'Yesterday was yesterday and today is today.' But there is more for you to consider than the friendship between an Isleta boy and an Anglo boy. You have listened to Renaldo and Ramon. Their stories speak for themselves.''

His voice was tiring, but he knew where to fire his final shot. ''Señor Lujan, you are a man of great insight. I know you will be wise in your decision. I thank you for your patience with an old man.''

Chairman Sylvan Lujan's chest swelled with such pride that it seemed his shirt would rip open. Mustering all the authority he could command he said, ''Martino! Do you *still* insist that your petition is valid?''

Martino stepped forward. Just as forcefully, he said, ''My petition is valid.''

Chairman Lujan's jaw dropped. It was plain to all that to be caught in a conflict between the esteemed old *vaquero* and the respected young *vaquero* was not a prospect the chairman relished. ''Ah . . . well . . .'' he sputtered.

''No matter,'' Martino said. He looked at my grandfather. ''My request displeases the man I honor more than any other. I withdraw my petition.''

Chairman Lujan slapped the table hard with his hand. ''Done!'' he exclaimed, before anyone could object.

As one, the board members nodded their agreement.

I turned from the window and sat on the ground, exhausted. ''*Madre de Dios*,'' I uttered beneath my breath. ''*Gracias*.''

When the last truck pulled away from our yard I

went into the house. Grandpa was seated at the kitchen table, sipping coffee—this time from his cup. My mother sat near him. I suspected that she had suggested that Grandpa find some way to help me. But it was the grand old man himself who had masterminded the coup. I took a jar of grape juice from the fridge and filled a glass. "I finished the chores."

"Uh-huh," Mama said.

I took a drink of juice. "How'd the board meeting go?"

Grandpa snorted. "Oh? You could not hear well enough with your ear pressed so hard against the screen?"

I sputtered and spilled grape juice down my shirt. Then we all laughed.

My mother said, "Someone will have to take the palomino back to Mr. Callister."

"I'll do it!" I said. "Oh . . . but would they let me?"

"Well, you're just a boy," my mother said. "But perhaps you know someone who could persuade them."

I looked at Grandpa in anticipation.

With infuriating nonchalance he took his good time in savoring the few remaining sips of his coffee. At last he pushed the cup aside. "On your feet, boy," he said, his leathery face creased into a smile. "Martino's waiting at his corral. You have a ride to make."

"*Ole!*" I shouted.

I rushed out the door to take Cheyenne home.

Chapter 7

On the last Monday in April, Steven went home. After school let out that day I rode over to see him. He was propped up in a rented hospital bed. The bed was in the den, just inside a wide sliding glass door that opened onto the back patio. In case of fire, it could be rolled straight out of the house. On a narrow harvest table, between the bed and the wall, were his AM/FM stereo, a stack of tapes and discs, a color TV with remote control, and another control unit that raised or lowered the bed.

"Welcome home, Amigo," I said, grasping his hand.

"Yeah," he said without smiling. His grip was still strong, but he looked like hell. He was down twenty pounds, at least. The wound over his right temple was still puffy. He was encased in a cast that extended from his waist down across both hips and thighs, then down his right leg to his ankle. There was a small opening at the crotch for bedpan purposes. His chest and shoulders were bare, and would remain that way by choice for as long as he was bed-ridden.

In a stupid attempt to make a joke I said, "Looks like you're wearing cement pants, man."

"Tell me about it," he snapped.

The TV was tuned to a game show. He pushed a button to raise the head of the bed, then grabbed the overhead bar and tried to lift himself into a more comfortable position. I knew better than to try and help. "Oh, shit!" he said, and lay back in frustration. With an angry jab he turned off the TV.

I stared at the floor in silence.

After a moment he said, "Look . . . Dave . . . I don't mean to take it out on you."

"I know."

It had been like that for the past couple of weeks. Up one moment, down the next. I kept telling him how sorry I was . . . how guilty I felt . . . how I'd do anything to make it up to him . . . how I wished it was me lying there instead of him.

"Well, that's just plain stupid," he said, switching it all around again. "It was my idea in the first place, remember?"

And so it went.

Now, on his first day home, I suspected that his irritation was heightened by the scene just beyond that sliding glass door—the corral, Tammy and Sundance, the open mesa, the Manzanos—symbols of freedom that mocked his confinement.

Another complaint was an infuriating itch on his leg where the wound was healing inside the cast. Frustrated, he slapped the cast repeatedly, unable to get at the irritation. "It's driving me nuts!"

On my way home that afternoon, I stopped at the 7-Eleven in Bosque Farms and bought a heavy-gauge wire coat hanger and a soft toothbrush. That night in the workshop of our barn, I untwisted the hanger, hammered it out on the anvil into a single straight piece, then tied the toothbrush to one end with saddle-stitching thread. Next day I gave the makeshift scratcher to Steven.

57

His eyes lit up. He grabbed it and shoved the brush inside the cast. "Oh, God . . . thanks . . . thanks," he said as he worked the wire back and forth with vigor.

Finally, I felt good about something.

One afternoon a rider appeared on the low bluff overlooking the Rio Grande, the boundary between the reservation and the Callister ranch. The rider started down the hill toward the house.

"Who the hell is that?" Steven asked.

At that distance I couldn't make out the rider any better than he could. But I knew who it was. None of my people would take that route to the Callister ranch. And there was only one Anglo who'd be so bold as to cross the reservation to do it. Soon, the rider's flamered tresses came into view. "Hey!" Steven exclaimed, and his face lit up like Christmas.

Brenda Cole tied Maude to the hitching post in the corral and took something out of her saddle bag. When she got to the patio, I slid the door open for her.

"Hi, David," she said in passing, then walked right up to Steven and bent down and planted a saucy kiss on his cheek. "I got a present for you," she told him.

"Another one?" I quipped.

Steven turned three shades of red.

"Shut up, David," Brenda said. But she smiled to show she wasn't really annoyed.

I stuck out my tongue at her, then got her a chair from the kitchen. She had a brown paper sack in her hand. She sat down, opened the sack and took out a book, and handed it to Steven. He looked at it, puzzled. "English Lit?"

She nodded. "I talked to Mr. Montoya about your grades." Mr. Montoya was the principal of Los Lunas High.

"He says you're doing well enough in everything else to take finals when the rest of us do. But you've

58

got to bone up on English literature, else you might flunk it.''

Steven moaned. "I hate English lit.''

"Sure you do—you and your rowdy friends who don't know a book from a cow pod." She shot me a meaningful look and I studied the light fixture on the ceiling. "Well, like it or not, you're going to do what Mr. Montoya says. I've written out the assignments." She showed him the sheet of tablet paper tucked inside the flyleafs. "You're to read one of these chapters every day, then answer the questions about it in the back of the book. Just to make sure you do it, I'm going to come by every couple of days and test you."

"Oh . . . yeah?"

"You better believe it."

He looked at the book with renewed interest, and I knew that my friend had developed a sudden fondness for English literature.

We talked through the rest of that afternoon: who was trying to get it on with whom at school; what songs would make it to the top of the charts. It was inevitable that we'd get to that day the three of us met by chance on the mesa.

"What about that bare-assed retreat, man," I prompted with a throaty chuckle.

"With Brenda in hot pursuit," Steven added.

"*Close* pursuit," Brenda corrected him.

We talked about the water tank, Brenda's teasing, Steven's buck naked retrieval of his clothes, her hasty withdrawal behind the piñon.

Brenda shot Steven a brazen look. "I should have stood my ground."

"Damn good thing you didn't," he retorted, leaving a hint of juicy consequence hanging in the air.

"Ha!" she exclaimed.

We tried to keep it going that way, Brenda and I.

59

We brought up favorite recollections, and upbeat things to keep it cheerful. It worked, until Brenda mentioned the trail ride.

"In October, on the Rocking C," she explained. "It's always a fun affair . . . huh, David?"

I confirmed that indeed it was.

She continued: "There'll be barrel racing, rodeo competition. There'll also be a chuck wagon barbeque that night with lots of fireworks, and a band with dancing. My grandfather goes all out every year. You'll be up and riding by then, easy."

Steven's face went blank and he turned his eyes to the ceiling. "I . . . I don't know."

The tone of his voice set off alarm bells inside my head. I didn't understand why then. It would be weeks before I would. Now, I tried to get things back on track. "Hey, Amigo . . . Wake up. You just been asked for a date, man. Better move quick or you know who will—Bulldog."

"Oh, David!" Brenda slapped me so hard on the shoulder I almost fell off the chair. "I'd just as soon go with *you* as with that scuz bucket."

I stood and made an exaggerated bow. "Well, excu-u-u-u-se me-e-e!" I sat back down. "You're too late though. I got other plans for that bash."

"Uh-huh. Rosie Barnes, right? I see you sucking up to her in study hall." She shot me a knowing look and started a teasing singsong: "*She laid the cornerstone of knowledge—in fact the whole damned college . . .*"

"Oh, stuff it, Brenda!" And it was my turn to go three shades of red.

Our antics got Steven's eyes away from the ceiling. But the spirit of our earlier banter was gone.

After awhile Brenda stood to go. "Don't forget, a chapter a day. I'll be by to check up on you."

He nodded.

She leaned over the bed and kissed him good-bye, and this time it wasn't on the cheek. "We'll talk about the trail ride later. Just . . . get well, hear?"

When she told me good-bye her eyes signaled that she sensed the same uneasiness I felt.

I stayed until it was dark, then made my farewell with the usual questions. Anything I could do? Anything I could bring? Anybody he wanted to come see him? Steven shook his head to every suggestion, saying nothing.

I gave him a friendly punch on the shoulder. "*Mañana*, Amigo."

I started for the sliding door, still disturbed by the bad vibes I couldn't get a handle on.

"David."

I turned. "Yeah?"

He was staring at the ceiling again. "There *is* one favor . . ."

"Anything, Amigo. Name it."

"Let the hawks go."

I thought I'd heard him wrong. "Say what?"

"The hawks. Turn them loose. It's cruel . . . wild creatures . . . caged up like that."

I didn't need a shrink to explain what brought that exchange on. The reason was right there in front of me, and the cage was plaster.

I'd promised to do anything. But . . . my prize hawks? I said, "Look . . . you sure? They'll make fine hunters. We'll have a lotta of fun with 'em . . . someday."

He rolled his head on the pillow and looked straight at me. "For me, Dave . . . okay?"

What could I say? I nodded. "Yeah . . . okay. For you, Amigo."

But it was one promise I had no intention of keeping.

Chapter 8

A joke making the rounds at Los Lunas High in those days was about this poor guy who was down on his luck. One day he hears a voice: "Cheer up—things could be worse." So he cheers up. And sure enough, things got worse.

I always think of that guy when I recall what happened next in Steven's life.

First, I have to explain something about horses. You can start a fight in almost any bar in the Rio Grande Valley talking this way. But truth is, most horses are just plain dumb. Take grazing. You can put them in a pen with two tons of the sweetest, highest quality hay, theirs for the taking, but let them spot a sprig of grass on the other side of the fence and they'll tear the fence down trying to get to it.

Tammy was like that. Mr. Callister bought the pinto mare for Steven the day after the family moved into their new home. That same afternoon she broke down the corral fence leaning over it to nibble at the alfalfa pasture on the other side. Next morning, Steven and his dad drove to Montgomery Ward in Albuquerque and got a roll of copper wire and some ceramic insulators. They strung a single strand around the top of the fence and electrified it with a six-volt battery. Then they hosed down the ground just inside the fence until it was deep mud and retreated to a corner of the corral to watch Tammy learn her lesson. Sure enough, in a couple of minutes, she started toward the fence.

That was the morning Pastor Atwood, the local Baptist minister, and his wife chose to call on the new family in the district. Spotting Steven and his father out back, the Atwoods skirted the house and went straight to the corral. The pastor extended his hand in introduction just as Tammy, grounded forelock-deep in mud, stretched her neck toward the forbidden greener pastures beyond the electrified fence. There was a sudden 'Crack!' as a bolt of charged ions arced four-inches outward from the wire, zapping Tammy high up on one moist nostril. More terrified than pained, the little mare squealed, leaped straight up into the air, extended all four legs in different directions and let an enormous fart that Steven swore could have been heard as far away as Santa Fe. Propelled by the great blast, particles of digested hay and oats rained down on everyone, redefining the pattern of Mrs. Atwood's white cotton dress with a pungent speckled hue. No one ever saw that dress again. It's a story still told up and down the Rio Grande Valley.

Add to it that Tammy learned her lesson. From that day on, there was no more eating over the fence. Until one Saturday the following year, a month after Steven came home from the hospital.

Steven told me what happened before I got there that day. It had been raining hard since dawn and he'd napped off and on between studying English lit. Just before noon the rain stopped and he was awakened by a strange sound coming from the corral. Then it struck him. It wasn't a sound—it was the *absence* of a sound. He knew at once what it was. Battery-charged electric fences operate intermittently. Each time the juice flows through the wire the battery emits a barely audible "thunk" to let you know it's still working. It's an easy sound to ignore, until it quits. During the downpour, the battery had gone dead.

Steven raised the bed for a better view. Sure enough, one section of fence near the barn was bent almost to the ground. Tammy had also detected the absence of that "thunk" and knew what it meant. Sometime during the morning hours she'd taken advantage of it.

She wasn't near the fence now. She was standing in the center of the corral with her neck arched low, her head almost touching the ground. While Steven watched, she took a few halting steps, then fell. Hard. As if her legs had turned to rubber. She struggled to rise, but couldn't.

Steven called for his father.

I had extra chores at home that morning and got to Steven's house about noon, just as Doc Greene, the veterinarian, drove into the driveway in his specially equipped GMC Suburban. That wasn't unusual. Doc Greene had been a vet for forty years and made it a point to keep in frequent touch with ranchers in the valley. Like a circuit-riding minister, he was always dropping by for one reason or another, mostly to immunize stock, sometimes just to chat. I figured it was something like that today. Then I spotted Mr. Callister leaning over Tammy where she lay in the corral, and I knew that Doc Greene's visit today was more serious.

I looped Sundance's reins over the front hitching post and followed Doc Greene to the corral. Tammy was lying on her side, thrashing her legs in the mud. Mr. Callister had locked Cheyenne and the other family horses in their stalls and was now trying to calm the downed mare. Tammy's eyes were glazed and her lips were drawn back, exposing her gums and teeth in a death's-head grin, like the tattoos I'd seen on the arms of some guys who'd served in Vietnam. She was in great pain. Doc Greene took one look, opened his bag and started filling a large hypodermic syringe. "What happened, Jess?"

Mr. Callister nodded toward the broken fence. "She got a belly fulla wet alfalfa, Hugh. Foundered her, for sure."

Doc Greene shoved the long needle deep into Tammy's neck and emptied whatever was in the syringe into her. In a couple of minutes she quit thrashing so hard, but her legs continued to twitch. Doc Greene knelt and ran his hands over her bloated stomach and up between her flanks, probing different places. After a full five minutes of prodding and tapping and listening to Tammy's innards through his stethoscope, he stood and shook his head. "Not good, Jess. She's all knots inside. We best put her under."

At those chilling words, I looked toward the house. Mr. Callister looked too. Just inside the sliding glass door, barely twenty-five yards away, Steven lay propped high, watching everything. His mother was standing at his side. Mr. Callister paused a moment, then looked back at Tammy. "She got any chance at all, Hugh?"

Doc Greene followed our glances toward the house. He took a deep breath and let it out slowly. "Well, I can't promise anything, understand . . . David, go fetch that big aluminum case outa the back of my carryall." He started rolling up his sleeves. "Jess, I'm gonna need hot water . . . lots of it. Tell Milli to fill all her pots and pans and keep 'em going on the stove."

"I'll tell her," I said. I ran and got Doc Greene's case then went to the house and told Mrs. Callister about the hot water. She went to the kitchen. I pulled a chair close to Steven's bed where I could watch with him. Without taking his eyes from the corral he said,

"She's not gonna make it." His voice was flat, emotionless, under tight control.

"No way," I argued. "Doc Greene's a great vet. You'll see."

For the remainder of that afternoon, working without let up, Doc Greene and Mr. Callister ministered to the stricken mare, rendering repeated hot, soapy enemas in hope of disentangling knotted intestines that were blocked as solidly as if they were filled with cement. Every so often, Doc Greene administered additional shots of antibiotics and sedatives. One to fight infection, the other to fight pain. From time to time Mrs. Callister called me to take a steaming kettle to the corral. Other times she took it herself. She'd changed into jeans and boots, and more than once she knelt in the mud to help with the mare's treatments. She wasn't squeamish. She was a cowboy's wife. She'd been through ordeals like this before.

Four hours into the treatment, Doc Greene got Tammy to her feet.

"Way to go!" I cried.

"Yeah!" Steven replied.

Doc Greene slipped a rope halter over Tammy's drooping head and urged her to take a few steps. Her legs wobbled and it was difficult for her to lift her hooves, but she walked about ten feet. Then her legs collapsed and she fell again, hard, and rolled onto her side. Doc Greene knelt and felt the artery at her neck for a moment, then gave her another shot. Then he resumed the treatment.

Around five o'clock, Mrs. Callister brought Steven and me a couple of baloney sandwiches and a can of Pepsi apiece. She'd remembered to make my sandwich with mustard. I didn't like mayonnaise, which was all Steven ever wanted on a sandwich. I thanked her and she said I was welcome, then she got another kettle

66

of hot water and carried it out the sliding glass door to the corral.

I took a bite of my sandwich.

Mrs. Callister had just entered the gate when her husband stood and looked at her and shook his head. She set the kettle on the ground. For a full minute she and the two men looked down at Tammy in silence. Then Mr. Callister went to the barn and returned with a tarpaulin and covered the little mare's still form. It was over.

The bite of sandwich in my mouth turned to sawdust. I looked at Steven, but couldn't get a word out. Jaw set, he swallowed hard several times and kept his eyes glued on the corral. He didn't make a sound.

Mrs. Callister came to the house. Her clothes were soiled with mud. Her face, always so pretty, now bore the strain of this new ordeal. Blurry eyed, she laid a hand on Steven's bare arm. "They did everything they could. I'm so—"

Before she could finish, Steven said, "Mom . . . don't let Dobbs Mills have her. Please." It was a plea from the heart.

Dobbs Mills was a slaughter house on old Route 66, east of Albuquerque, that manufactured pet food. They would remove dead stock free of charge from anywhere within fifty miles of their processing plant. They used every part of the carcass in their products, except the hide. They auctioned the hides to tanners. For most ranchers, getting rid of dead stock like that was a good deal.

Mrs. Callister studied her son for a moment, then went back to the corral where her husband was helping Doc Greene pack his equipment. She said something and Mr. Callister looked back at the house, then nodded. After Doc Greene left, Mr. Callister went to the barn. We heard a rough engine start up, and a moment later he came out driving the old Ford tractor he used for earth-moving work around the ranch. It was equipped with a back-hoe and scoop. For the next hour, after stopping once to switch on the corral flood-lights, he dug a wide, deep hole right next to where Tammy lay. Then he eased the scoop under Tammy's body and nudged it across the ground until it slid into the hole with the tarp still covering her. He dozed the dirt back into the hole and tamped it down hard with the scoop, then drove the tractor back and forth over the grave until the mound was almost flat again. After another good rain, it would be. I couldn't help but think how similar it was to the ancient burials of my ancestors, who were wrapped in their finest blankets and entombed in the dirt floor at Saint Augustine Church.

Mr. Callister returned the tractor to the barn and came into the house. His clothes, too, were encrusted with mud. He stood at the foot of Steven's bed for a moment, then said, "She'll always be at home."

Steven nodded, but said nothing.

Then the onetime world-champion cowboy added: "We'll find you another good horse, soon as you're up and about."

Suddenly it was like the trail ride conversation with Brenda all over again. Steven fixed his eyes on the ceiling and that same strange look that had set off alarm bells in me before clouded his countenance. He shook his head slowly on the pillow. "I don't want another horse. Ever."

Mr. Callister gave his son's foot a pat through the sheet. "We'll talk about it later." He went to clean up while Mrs. Callister fixed him something to eat.

Thinking back on that scene later, I could understand Mr. Callister's dismissal of evidence that should have caused concern. He was certain that Steven's forlorn comment about not wanting another horse stemmed from the grief of the moment. I thought so too, at first. Then I remembered that I'd heard that same tone in his voice long before Tammy got sick, and I wasn't so sure.

When we were alone Steven said, "Look . . . David . . . I wanta get some sleep . . . I . . . I . . ."

His voice choked off and his eyes clouded and he bit his lip until it turned white. Then he rolled his face toward the wall and his body shook with sobs.

There was nothing I could say. I took his untouched sandwich off the bed and put it on the table beside his Pepsi. Then I switched off the light and left.

Late that night I slipped out of bed and went to the wire cage behind my house. I lifted the two young hawks down from their perch and carried them out into the yard. I held them close for a moment. "Goodbye, pretty birds," I said. Then, holding them high, I gave them a gentle push into the still air.

For a long moment, unaccustomed to limitless space, they circled higher and higher into the moonlit night. At last getting their bearings, they tilted their wings and soared away toward Black Mesa.

Caged no more . . . free again.

Chapter 9

In May, Miss Adkins, the home-visiting teacher at Los Lunas High, went to the Callister Ranch to give Steven his final exams on the same days the rest of us took them at school. Despite being absent from classes since March, he made a respectable C in every subject except one. In English lit he made an A. It surprised Miss Adkins, it surprised the teaching staff at Los Lunas High, and it surprised the whole freshman class. It didn't surprise me. I knew the red-headed incentive that had kept him glued to the English lit text day and night.

Two weeks after exams, the long awaited emancipation day arrived. Wednesday morning, the first day of June, paramedics loaded Steven into an ambulance and took him back to Saint Anne's, where orthopedists cut the cast from his body and stood him on his feet for the first time in three months. He promptly fainted. The doctors revived him with smelling salts, then tried again, supporting him on each side. He took a few wobbly steps, rested, then took a few more. By next afternoon he had graduated to crutches, a full day ahead of most people recovering from similar injuries.

On Friday, Mrs. Callister drove to Albuquerque and brought him home. During that first week out of the cast he walked around the house on crutches. The second week he ventured out on short walks around the yard without them. Responding to the walks and the three-times-a-day exercises prescribed by therapists, the weakened muscles rebounded and the lost weight returned. By the end of the month Steven was walking three to five miles a day along the irrigation ditch between the ranch and the reservation. Most times I was with him. Sometimes we'd stop by the barn and he'd look over the fence at the spot where Tammy lay buried. But not once did he enter the corral.

On the Fourth of July, Brenda and I threw a surprise party for him. Late that morning she and I "just happened to" show up at the ranch at the same time. She, Steven and I sat on the front porch in the enormous wicker chairs his parents had brought up from Juarez. Brenda and I played it cool, bringing Steven up to date on the latest gossip, as if this were no more than another routine visit.

Just before noon, a dozen riders rounded the big bend on Highway 47 and came galloping hell-bent-for-leather down the dirt road toward the ranch. Steven sat forward in his chair. "What the . . . ?"

Bill and Jim Kagy and their sister, Rebecca, leading the pack on Thunder, Tumbleweed, and Preacher were the first in recognizable view. Then came Eddy Gomez on his black gelding, Domino, and Cindy Lewis on her brown-and-white pinto, Patches. One by one other riders and mounts became recognizable. Off to one side the Boyd twins, independent as ever, roared along on their matching red-and-white Honda motorcycles.

Steven stood up. "Hey, those are guys from school."

"Well, I'll be damned," I said.

"How 'bout that?" Brenda added.

71

"Yeah, how 'bout that?" Steven echoed, and shot us a wry grin.

Without slowing, the pack turned onto the lane in front of the house and rode right up to the hitching post just outside the front yard. "Ayy, Steve, ole buddy!" a foghorn voice called out. "Let's party!"

I gave Brenda a look that needed no words: *Who the hell invited that goon?* She shrugged and I knew that she was as surprised as I was. It was a stupid question anyway. No one *had* to invite Bulldog Jenkins anywhere. He just showed up, like fungus between your toes. Now here he was, acting like he was the best pal Steven ever had, and the hairs on the back of my neck tingled an ominous warning. Then I spotted raven-haired Rosie Barnes in hip-hugging jeans and figured that the day held promise after all.

In on things from the start, Steven's parents had set up the back patio while we kept him occupied on the front porch. There were tables loaded with nachos and cold-cuts, a charcoal grill for cooking burgers and hot dogs, thermoses of lemonade, and iced-down cans of Pepsi and Mountain Dew.

The party got going full swing. Jim and Rebecca Kagy claimed a side yard and challenged all comers at horseshoes. In the driveway, Bill Kagy led the cheering as the Boyd twins vied to see who could pop the longest wheelie on their bikes. Cindy Lewis tuned her ghetto blaster to high decibel, and on the patio Eddy Gomez broke into his imitation of Twisted Sister, accompanying himself on an air guitar. Everyone stuffed their faces.

Rosie Barnes and I filled our plates and took a couple of folding chairs to a quiet corner of the yard to get better acquainted. We no sooner got seated when something distracted me. Side-by-side in the patio glider, Steven and Brenda were carrying on a spirited

72

conversation, accented by frequent laughs and much entwining of hands. That part was fine. What wasn't fine was Bulldog. Leaning against the corral fence, he kept his beady eyes glued to Steven like a puma stalking prey. If Steven noticed, he paid it no mind. I did. It was a dark cloud in an otherwise sunny sky, and it worried me so much that when Rosie suggested we find a more private spot up in the barn loft I shook my head.

Rosie's dark eyes flashed. "Well! If that's the way you feel, David Baca." She rose in a huff.

I grabbed her arm. "Aw, c'mon, Rosie . . . sit down, please. It's something else . . . honest."

I must have convinced her. She dropped back in the chair and looked at me, puzzled. I nodded toward Bulldog.

She glanced toward the fence. "Oh, David, you don't have to worry about Bulldog and me. That's been over for eons."

I smiled. "Naw, it's not that, Rosie. It's them." I motioned toward the swing. "Bulldog's been looking poison darts at Steven ever since he got here."

Rosie looked at Bulldog again. "Yeah . . . see what you mean. He's still pissed about that school bus scene, you know."

"It figures."

"He's got one on for Brenda, too."

"So what else is new?"

"Fat chance he's got is all I can say." After a moment she added, "You know he's telling everyone that Steven's scared of horses now."

"Say what?"

"Really freaked out, Bulldog says."

"Oh, bull. What a crock of . . ."

Memory cut me short. It all came back to me: Steven's weird reaction that afternoon Brenda brought up the trail ride. That blank stare at the ceiling the night Tammy died and his father promised him another horse. *I don't want another horse. Ever.* Now I understood the alarm bells that went off in my head on those occasions. Bulldog was right!

"Hey, Dave! You bring your stopwatch?"

I looked up to see Tommy Boyd yelling at me from across the yard. I shook my head.

"I did!" Eddy Gomez yelled back.

"*Barrel race!*" Tommy shouted.

Jim and Rebecca Kagy were already setting up the barrels in the training arena adjacent to the corral. Others were leading their horses to the starting line, tightening cinches, checking leather.

I glanced at Steven. His face was blank. I uttered a prayer beneath my breath.

Rosie jumped to her feet. "Get Sundance," she said, excited.

Barrel racing was the favorite competition in the valley. A race against time around three barrels arranged in a triangle about a hundred feet apart, it required good horsemanship, close coordination between mount and rider, and just plain luck. Starting near the base of the triangle, the rider first must circle the right or left barrel as he chooses, race to and circle the other barrel at the base, race to and circle the remaining barrel at the top of the triangle, then race back across the starting line. A good run is seventeen to eighteen seconds. Twenty seconds is sad-city. Fifteen to sixteen usually takes top prize. Last fall in the freshman rodeo at Los Lunas High, Steven and Tammy had run away with it in fourteen and a half seconds. The record was still standing.

I decided not to compete.

"Chicken!" Rosie accused me. Then, "Can I borrow Sundance, then? He's a lot faster'n my nag."

"Sure."

She ran to get him ready.

Steven and Brenda came to the fence just outside the arena. I could tell by her expression that she'd guessed what I already knew. I went and stood with them.

At the end of the first heat, Bulldog and his ebony gelding, Blackie, held the lead at sixteen seconds. Eddy Gomez on Domino took second with sixteen and a half. Rosie and Sundance stood third at seventeen. I winced. Sundance was better than that.

"She's over-reining him," Steven said.

"Yeah," I agreed.

Rosie must have realized it too. On the second heat she let Sundance have his head. He spun the turns so tight that Rosie's leg brushed the barrels. They crossed the finish line in fifteen and a half seconds, beating Bulldog by half a second.

Bulldog smoldered. It didn't take a lot of smarts to read what was on his mind. To lose was bad enough, but to lose to a girl!

By the end of the sixth heat, Rosie and Bulldog were tied three to three. One by one the other riders dropped out. With only two competitors left, a seventh and final heat was called to decide the winner. Bulldog was sullen. Rosie beamed.

Then Steven made a mistake. "Go Rosie!" he yelled.

Others took up the chant.

"Yea—Go Rosie!"

"Show him what for, Rosie!"

"ROSIE . . . ROSIE . . . ROSIE!"

It was too much for Bulldog. Jumping from the saddle, he stalked through the gate and walked right up to Steven. "You so anxious to see me bite dust,

75

Callister . . . mount up. I'll ride your ass inta the ground.''

Steven lowered his eyes, saying nothing.

I stepped between them. ''Aw, c'mon, Bulldog . . . it's just a ga—''

Bulldog splayed a ham-size hand against my chest and pushed me aside like I was a rag doll. ''Keep outa this, Injun.''

Leaden silence. Steven's face was ashen. Bulldog knew he'd struck a raw nerve. Encouraged, he egged on the others. ''How 'bout it guys? Callister and me, one on one. Best time in one heat wins. He can even ride my horse, all fair and square.''

Tommy Boyd was first to respond. ''Go get him, Steven,'' he enthused.

''Yeah, Steven,'' agreed Eddy Gomez. ''Show him how a real champ does it.''

Steven shook his head. If he was trying to talk, words wouldn't come.

''Yeah . . . *Champ*,'' Bulldog sneered, his voice pure sarcasm now, ''show me how it's done.'' He grabbed the front of Steven's shirt and started pulling him toward the corral.

Misreading Steven's reluctance, Tommy and Eddy took positions on either side of him, grasped his elbows, and helped Bulldog maneuver him toward the gate.

In tears now, Brenda tried to hold on to Steven. ''Tommy . . . Bulldog . . . you guys . . . stop it!''

Bulldog laughed, but there was no mirth in him.

Brenda looked at me, pleading.

Sucking in a deep breath, I crossed myself and whispered, ''*Madre de Dios*, help me now'' and shoved my way through the throng toward Bulldog. I'd almost reached him when Steven folded his arms across his own chest and gripped his shoulders, as if hugging himself.

What?

All of a sudden Steven released his grip and plunged his elbows straight back into Tommy's and Eddy's chests with such force that it sent them sprawling. They rolled on the ground, gasping for breath.

Hand still clamped to Steven's shirt, Bulldog turned just in time to see the blow coming. In the next instant his nose and mouth erupted in a bloody pulp as Steven's fist smashed into his face, squashing it as one might squash a rotten tomato.

There was a collective gasp from the crowd.

I froze.

The blow would have felled a mule. But Bulldog was still on his feet!

Stunned, he stood for a long moment with his head drooping, like a wounded toro. Then he raised his hand to his face, withdrew it and looked at the blood in disbelief. Eyes ablaze with hatred, he erupted in fury. "You . . . Son-of-a-bitch!" Arms outstretched he dove headlong at Steven, grasped him around the throat and began choking him.

"Bulldog! No!" Someone yelled.

"Stop it! Stop it! Stop it!" Brenda screamed over and over while pounding Bulldog on the back.

Jim Kagy and I grabbed Bulldog's arms and tried to break his grip. It was like trying to bend forged steel.

Steven's hands dropped straight down in front of him, a sign he was losing consciousness. In full panic now, I clawed at Bulldog's arm. All of a sudden Steven clasped his hands together and thrust them straight up between Bulldog's wrists. Bulldog's vise-like grip broke and his arms went flying to either side. Without pause, Steven brought his still-clasped hands down

77

with all his might onto Bulldog's nose. The blow bent Bulldog double. Completing the surprise maneuver, Steven brought his left knee up hard into Bulldog's chin, lifting him off his feet and hurling him backward onto the ground.

With a pathetic moan, Bulldog rolled off his back and pushed himself up on his hands and knees. I couldn't believe there was fight left in him.

Fists tight, panting for breath, Steven stood beside the fallen bully, waiting for him to rise. Bulldog looked up at Steven for a moment, then lowered his head and shook it slowly.

It was over.

No one knew what to do.

I went over and put a hand on Steven's shoulder. "Hey, man . . ."

He shoved my hand away. Then without a word he retreated to the house and slammed the door behind him.

Eddy Gomez helped Bulldog onto his horse and the two of them rode off in silence. The Boyd twins roared off on their Hondas. One by one the others mounted and departed in the same forlorn way. I started toward the house, but Brenda stopped me. "Not now, David. He's hurt . . . in more ways than one. He'll need us later. But not now."

"She's right," Rosie agreed. She and Brenda mounted their horses and waited.

For a long moment I stared at the house in thought, trying to find some meaning for what had happened here today. After awhile I mounted Sundance, and Brenda and Rosie and I rode away together. Brenda was right. Steven *would* need us later.

But I wasn't about to wait for him to figure it out.

Chapter 10

For as long as I could remember, my grandfather's room was a world apart—an enchanted place of enticing smells and sights and things. Shelves on two walls held silver trophies, jeweled belts and medallions, and other awards for riding and roping skills, some dating from shortly after the turn of the century. Atop an ancient roll-top desk was a mason jar filled with thin black cigars from Tijuana, sealed in with a cinnamon stick and apple peels for flavor. Near the fireplace were two high-back, cane rocking chairs that Grandpa had designed and had made in Mexico. The brick floor was covered with a timeworn red-and-black wool rug that had been hand dyed and woven on the Big Reservation by Navajo craftsmen. Dominating all was a huge double bed, carved from a Manzano Mountain pine by Grandpa himself over a half-century before as a present to his bride, my grandmother. In this bed my father was born, my grandmother died, and, until I became too old for such things, I had often lain at night with my head cradled in Grandpa's arm, listening to tales of an era that I could never know.

It was to this room, late on the night following the aborted Fourth of July party, that I came to the past in hope of shaping the future.

I knocked on the door.

"Hmmmmpphh!" That was Grandpa's invitation to come in.

He was bent forward in one of the rockers, lighting a cigar with a taper from the fireplace. This was the first year Grandpa had kept a fire during summer. While the rest of us complained of the July heat, he wrapped a heavy wool serape over his flannel robe each night and complained of the cold. Miguel and I made sure his log box was always filled with piñon and cedar.

Grandpa blew out the taper, laid it to smolder on the stone hearth and waved for me to enter. I settled into the other rocker and watched smoke from his cigar swirl above his head, thinking how closely it matched the color of his hair.

I rocked in silence, staring into the amber flames. The cedar log crackled, sending forth a pungent aroma that I'd always found pleasant. After a while, without looking at me, Grandpa said, "Something is troubling you." It was a statement, not a question.

"Yes."

"Things are not going well in school?"

The question worried me. I'd been out of school for summer vacation since May, and wouldn't go back until September. Mama had mentioned a couple of times recently that Grandpa was "becoming confused." This was the first time I'd seen evidence of it.

"No, Grandpa, it's not that. It's . . . something else."

"Um-hum." The ash from his cigar dropped onto his lap. He brushed it onto the hearth and continued smoking. He would question me no further, I knew, until I was ready to discuss the problem.

Mounted on the wall above the fireplace were three

rows of framed photographs. All were of Grandpa as a young man, posed with some of the people who had shared the milestones of his life. I knew them only from what Grandpa had told me about them, or from history books. The largest photo was of Grandpa and an aging Teddy Roosevelt, taken in front of the governor's palace in Santa Fe during the ex-president's last journey west. There was one of Grandpa and Tom Mix taken on film location in California where Grandpa had choreographed stunt rides for the famous cowboy star. Grandpa and Buffalo Bill Cody in Denver, during the time Grandpa was helping the old scout stock the ranch given to him by the people of Colorado. Grandpa and Frank James . . .

I studied the photo of Grandpa and the notorious outlaw. "Grandpa . . . is it true that you picked out Frank James's horses for him?" I'd heard the story many times, but never tired of it.

Grandpa squinted at the photograph and nodded. "Fine mounts, too."

"And Jesse's?"

Grandpa shook his head. "No. Jesse was deep in his grave by then. After Jesse was shot, the fire went out of Frank. The railroad lawyers tried hard to have him sent to prison for all those robberies he and Jesse pulled off. But they couldn't find a jury anywhere in Missouri that would convict him. Frank went straight after that. Was making his living as a race starter when he got in touch with me. Was traveling around the country, county fairs and such . . ."

Grandpa frowned and spit a piece of tobacco onto the hearth. His cigar had gone out. He re-lit it, gave a couple of hearty puffs to make sure it was going good, then returned to the images etched so long ago in his memory. "People came to those fairs from all over, most of them just to see Frank James in person.

81

They would talk with him, get his autograph—he charged fifty cents for that—made sure their children got to touch him. It was show business, and Frank loved it. Bill Cody told him about me and he wrote and asked me to find a pair of blooded quarter horses for his personal use. I knew Frank's reputation well enough to guess what kind of mount would suit him. I located a pair of matched bays on the Crippled Tree spread down in Las Cruces and bought them for Frank. Delivered them to him myself. They were spirited, blue-ribbon blood lines . . . showoff mounts vain enough to match Frank's own personality. He was so taken with them that he doubled my fee. He rode those bay geldings right up until the day he died.''

"Matched his personality?" I said, feigning ignorance. It was as good a lead as I could think of to get to what I'd come for.

"Mighty important," Grandpa said. "Not every horse is for every rider. You must . . ." He hesitated and eyed me askance. "Why are you asking things I taught you long ago?"

I smiled, admitting deception. "Sorry, Grandpa."

He rocked a moment in silence. "You did not visit me tonight to hear stories about Frank James."

"No, Grandpa."

"Um-hum." He took a final drag on his cigar and tossed it into the fire. "So, are you going to tell what *is* troubling you?"

"It's my friend, Grandpa."

"The Anglo boy."

He knew me that well. "Yes," I replied.

I hadn't known how to explain it, but once I started, it poured from me in a torrent. I went all the way back to the hunt for Diablo: the broken rope, the giant horse falling on Steven, the hospital, the long months in the body cast, the slow healing, Tammy's tragic death,

Steven's reaction when the subject of riding came up, our walks together to strengthen his muscles, how he avoided the corral. Then I told about the bad scene at the picnic today, and how Bulldog, Tommy and Eddy had tried to force Steven onto a horse, and what Steven did to them. "He was like a madman, Grandpa. He beat Bulldog up something awful."

"Sounds like that was due," Grandpa said.

"Yeah. Steven's no coward, that's for sure. But he's scared now, Grandpa . . . scared to death of horses."

"With good reason," Grandpa said. "I've seen it in grown men, much less a boy."

That didn't help. "But, Grandpa . . . here in the valley . . . a guy not riding. He'll be left out. He won't have any friends left at all . . . well, he'll have me. But we won't be able to do anything . . . not like before."

"Um-hum."

"It's not fair, Grandpa. Steven is . . . was . . . a fine rider. You shoulda seen how he handled Cheyenne. What happened wasn't his fault. I'm the one who talked him into it. I feel so responsible—"

"It was the fault of a bad rope," Grandpa cut in.

"Bad rope, bad luck. Whatever you call it, he wouldn't have been there except for me."

This time he didn't try to put balm on it. Instead, he said, "And you want to do something to make up for it."

"I sure do."

"Like find him another horse."

We were almost there. "Yes."

"I understand. And you want me to tell you what kind of horse you should look for."

"Uh . . . not exactly."

His brow furrowed with even deeper lines and he looked at me, puzzled. "Then I do *not* understand."

I took a deep breath. "Grandpa, I came to ask if . . . if *you* would find a horse for Steven."

He stared at me blankly, then a look of such pain crossed his face that I felt alarmed. "Grandpa!"

He raised a hand to silence me.

I persisted, "Grandpa, I didn't mean to hurt you. I was only . . ."

"No . . . no. *You* have not hurt me. What hurts is what I must say to you." He looked all around the room. Then in a voice more forlorn than I'd ever heard it, he said, "This is my world now. You and Miguel, your parents—you are my only family. Ramon buys my food and my tobacco. Anna cooks my meals, washes and sews my clothes. You and Miguel keep my log box filled, and do any chores I ask." He sighed. "So much is done for me, while I . . . do so little."

With painful insight I realized that what I was hearing was not a new thought to him, and his lament tore at my heart. "Oh, Grandpa . . . that's not true. You . . . what about the stock council meeting last March . . . remember? You were great!"

If he was listening he made no sign of it. "Now you come to me worried about your friend and you ask for my help. And I must tell you that I cannot help. My eyes . . . I am no longer . . . capable . . ."

His voice trailed off. He pulled the serape tighter about his shoulders and sat staring into the fire.

I wondered what to say. Nothing I could think of seemed adequate. I stood and went to him. I bent down and kissed his weathered cheek. He nodded once, but said nothing.

I left.

Throughout the remainder of that long night I tossed on my bed, angry at myself for being so foolish. At dawn, bleary-eyed, I threw on my work clothes and

84

went to the kitchen and poured coffee into my cup instead of milk. It was something new and my mother was quick to notice it. "You didn't sleep well?" she asked.

"I didn't sleep, period." I dropped into my chair at the table and drank the coffee, black. It was a foreign taste, heavy and bitter, but I didn't care. "Papa already gone?" I asked. For the first month after Papa got out of bed he'd walked with a cane. Even now, he carried it with him sometimes when he rode.

My mother placed a huge ball of kneaded bread into a crock to rise, wiped her hands on her apron and got a pitcher of orange juice from the refrigerator. "South Mesa," she said. "Fence mending. He says for you to meet him at the pond gate, and to bring your tools. You're going to have to do most of the work."

She poured a glass of orange juice and set it on the table before me. "*Chorizos* or French toast?"

"French toast." I pushed away the coffee and grabbed the juice.

We heard Grandpa's door open and we both looked toward the hallway. Grandpa never rose this early anymore. He trudged into the kitchen in his slippers and robe, the serape still in place over his shoulders. When he didn't even glance my way the remorse of last night returned to torment me.

Grandpa asked, "Any more of that coffee, Anna?"

She poured him a cup and he brought it to the table. Instead of taking his usual chair, he sat down next to me. "Tell me more about this Anglo boy," he said. There was a strange new timbre in the old voice. "Everything. His likes and dislikes. How he does in school. How he gets along with his friends . . . with his parents. All you can tell me that will help me understand his personality."

85

I stopped the juice glass halfway to my mouth. "Grandpa! You're gonna do it?"

He placed a leathery hand atop mine. "One last time, Amigo. Because you ask."

Chapter 11

In the lengthy summer days that followed, I worked with my father on the pueblo rangelands from dawn to dusk, learning the *vaquero*'s trade. The fact that I was his son didn't sway Papa to cut me any slack when it came to chores. I was surprised at how much there was to do for cows, without ever having to come in contact with one. There were windmills to repair and lubricate, gates to re-hang, water tanks to clean, salt licks to replenish. Fence-mending was a never-ending chore. In spite of the long hours, there were compensations. Daytime temperatures in the high mountain pastures were always cooler than those in the valley. In July and August, that was reason enough to want to be there.

Often at sundown, instead of going home, I'd ride to the Callister's for dinner. I'd sit on the patio with Steven long into the evening. Sometimes Brenda would be there, too. On those occasions I'd look for clues from them whether they wanted me to stick around or not. When they did, we'd watch TV or listen to tapes or just talk long into the night. Sometimes we'd take a long walk around the ranch. Other times Steven and Brenda dropped hints that they wanted to take those moonlight strolls alone, and I'd split early. It was all friendly.

Steven's parents made it clear that Brenda and I were welcome to drop by anytime. In fact, they encouraged us. Following his fight with Bulldog, Steven had withdrawn more and more from his friends—from the valley life-style he'd once been so much a part of. His only visitors now were Brenda and me. His refusal to ride had made him an outsider to all the others.

One evening, the three of us sat together on the patio watching the Manzanos turn pink, then red, then purple in the glow of a brilliant sunset. It was a crazy-quilt patchwork of colors that never ceased to be awe-inspiring, no matter how often you saw it. But on this occasion it provoked a different reaction from Steven. With a faraway look in his eyes, he asked, "You ever come across that son of a bitch in your work up there?" There was bitterness and pain in his voice, so Brenda took his hand and pulled it into her lap.

I knew his rancor wasn't directed at me. "No," I replied. "But I will, Amigo. I promise you that. Someday I will. And he will be sorry when I do!"

"Oh, David!" Brenda protested.

Steven made no comment.

We let the subject drop. But I made a silent vow that someday I'd carry through on that promise.

As sad as the situation was with my friend, there was a flip side to the ill wind that was blowing in our lives. While Steven was withdrawing from life, at my home an even stranger transformation was taking place. Grandpa began to emerge from a twenty-year cocoon. The day after he questioned me about Steven's habits, Grandpa surprised everyone by rising at dawn to eat breakfast with the rest of us. Instead of his usual frayed robe and slippers, he was wearing his denim jeans and jacket, and rawhide boots. It was the first time I'd seen him fully dressed since the council meeting five months before. He transferred coffee from his cup to his saucer and blew on it. "Anna, will you drive me to Los Lunas after chores?"

My father almost choked on his *chorizo*. He began to sputter and cough.

Grandpa pushed Papa's water glass closer, and Papa grabbed it and took a big drink. Grandpa said, "Calm yourself, Ramon. We will not be gone long." With an impish grin, he sipped the coffee from his saucer.

Papa gave Mama a look of bewilderment. She returned it with one that signaled, *I'll explain it all later*. She said to Grandpa, "Yes, after the bread is in the ovens."

That night I learned from Mama that the trip to Los Lunas had been a bummer. Following Grandpa's directions, Mama had taken an unpaved back road to a ranch he had favored as a young *vaquero*. Trouble was, the ranch no longer existed. In its place, a drab development of identical little-box houses stretched along the river bottom. Distraught to see for himself how much of the world he had known was gone, Grandpa had complained that he should never have left his room. Mama saved the day. On the drive home she convinced him just to check with her before planning future trips. That way she could call ahead to make sure there'd be no more wild goose chases. Grandpa agreed.

Thereafter, a couple of times a week, Grandpa and Mama took off in her truck to check out another stock ranch in search of a horse for Steven. But nothing Grandpa saw suited him. Each night I'd ask Mama how it went, and each night she'd shake her head. One evening, after Grandpa and Mama had made a long and fruitless trip to Santa Fe, I asked Grandpa what kind of horse he was looking for.

"I don't know," he replied. "But I will when I see it."

One evening at the Callister's, out of Steven's ear-shot, I got around to telling Mr. Callister what my grandfather was doing. I'd been worried about that, what with Mr. Callister being a champion horseman himself and all. He thought about it for a moment, then said, "I've heard that Pete Baca once knew every horse in this valley by name. I guess if there *is* another horse out there for Steven, there's no better person than your grandpa to find it." Then he thanked me. From the way he said it I knew Steven's problem had been a heavy weight on his father's heart.

As summer waned, I became more and more dis-couraged. It was beginning to look like a lost cause. Then came the final Sunday in August.

That morning I slept late and missed going to church with my parents. Our family had a rule about that. Missing early mass meant make-up mass later in the day. So I attended noon mass at Saint Augustine alone, then rode straight to Steven's.

Mr. Callister came out of the house and walked over to the hitching post where I was tying Sundance. "Ste-ven's gone shopping with his mother," he said.

"Oh?" I started to untie the reins.

"Leave him hitched. Your mama called from Al-buquerque, said your grandpa wants to see me and you." His tan Chevy Blazer was parked in the drive-way. He fished a key from his pocket. "Come on."

It could only mean one thing. "Where're we meet-ing Grandpa?" I asked, elated.

"Dobbs Mills."

The bloom faded. "Dobbs Mills?"

"Makes no sense to me either," he confided. "But that's what the lady said."

The old slaughter plant was spread out over ten acres

of a shallow wooded valley in Tijeras Canyon. You didn't have to know where it was to find it. All you had to do was follow your nose. There were four warehouse-size brick buildings, each dedicated to a different role in the manufacture, canning, packing and shipment of pet food. All were closed this Sunday.

The slaughter house itself, recognizable by the two massive cement smokestacks rising from its roof, sat on the back side of the acreage far away from the other three buildings. It was surrounded on three sides by huge corrals, each subdivided into smaller stock pens. Usually full, on this weekend most of the pens were empty. The pen nearest to the slaughter house was known as the 'Judas pen'. From this final enclosure a 'friendly' mare, trained for the purpose, would lead the others to their deaths. I counted eleven horses of various shapes and sizes in the Judas pen. Most were old, sore-spotted and emaciated. All were destined for the boiling vats–when the plant opened at dawn tomorrow.

Mama's blue pickup was parked on the backside of the Judas pen. I pointed. ''There they are.''

Mr. Callister pulled up alongside the truck. Mama was sitting in the cab. She waved and nodded toward the pen. Grandpa was standing at the fence with a man I didn't recognize.

''That your grandpa?'' Mr. Callister asked.

The question made me realize that they'd never met. ''Yes.'' I was just as anxious as he was to see what this was all about. ''C'mon.''

I introduced Mr. Callister to Grandpa.

At the name ''Callister,'' the stranger grabbed Mr. Callister's hand and pumped it. ''Well I'll be damned . . . Jess Callister . . . recognize you from your pictures any day. Name's Brock . . . Ned Brock. I'm livestock buyer for the plant here. Sure an honor to meet the World Champion Cowboy.''

"Well . . . not anymore,'' Mr. Callister said. "But thanks all the same.'' He turned his attention back to Grandpa. "Well, Señor Baca?''

Grandpa pointed.

Alone in a far corner, shying away from the other horses, was a small black mare. Unlike the others, she was well proportioned and nicely filled out. Her smooth summer coat reflected the sun like polished ebony.

Mr. Callister shaded his eyes for a better view.

Ned Brock said, "Jess . . . I don't know what it is you're lookin' for, and you sure don't need any advice about horses from me . . . but I gotta say, you don't want that mare.''

"Oh?'' Mr. Callister said.

"Like I was tellin' the old gent here yesterday, these're slaughter horses . . . somethin' wrong with all of 'em. Now take that little black. She looks good and all, but somebody's mistreated her so bad her brain's all twisted. She's so spooky you just can't get close to her.''

Grandpa said nothing. His eyes were fixed on the mare.

"What's her name?'' Mr. Callister asked.

"Who knows?'' Ned Brock replied.

Mr. Callister stepped around the fence and approached the corner where the mare was standing. She spotted him and sidled nervously, trying to avoid him without getting close to the other horses. Mr. Callister stopped and studied her for a long moment. Then he frowned and came back to where Grandpa was still leaning on the fence. "*Señor*, I don't understand. What makes you believe that's the horse for me?''

Grandpa shook his head. "Not for you, *Señor*.'' He

pushed back from the fence and turned to look at Mr. Callister. *"For the boy."*

They stood like that, champion cowboy and old *vaquero*, eyes locked. Whatever understanding passed between them during those silent seconds remained their secret, for neither of them spoke of it afterward.

Mr. Callister turned to Ned Brock. "How much for that little black?"

Brock shook his head. "Well . . . she was goin' for four cents a pound for dog meat. Forty dollars and she's yours. But if you don't mind me sayin' so, Jess . . . you been outa the saddle too damned long."

Chapter 12

We took her home that day in a horse-trailer Mr. Callister borrowed from Ned Brock. We were backing into the corral when Mrs. Callister's green Coupe de Ville pulled into the driveway. She and Steven came around back to see what was going on.

I got out to close the corral gate and Mr. Callister stepped around to open the trailer. When he lowered the tailgate, the little black mare bolted out in a dead run straight toward the stables. Just as she got to the building, Cheyenne emerged from his stall. At the sight of the towering stallion, the little mare skidded to a stop, frantically looked around the corral, then retreated to a lonely corner behind the watering trough. Unsure which of us presented the greater threat, she stood watching every move we or the golden horse made.

At the fence, Steven pushed his grey Stetson back in amusement. "What, somebody tell me, is *that*?"

"Present for you," his father replied.

There was a moment for comprehension, then Steven's look of amusement disintegrated. He shook his head. "Uh-uh . . . no way."

Mr. Callister made no comment. Steven opened his mouth as if to say something else, but whatever it was didn't come out. Instead, he turned and went to the house. His mother and father exchanged pained looks, then Mrs. Callister followed her son.

I guess anyone else in my position would have left right then, but I didn't. During the long mending following Steven's accident I had come to feel almost as much a part of this family as my own. Now, I went to the patio, sat in the glider, and watched the little mare try to make herself invisible. Before long Steven came out the back door and dropped into a chair near by. He propped his feet up on the railing and looked out toward the corral. Voice sullen, he said, "Sure don't know why he did such a dumb thing as that."

"Well . . . I do." I told him about Grandpa and how I'd set the whole thing up weeks ago.

He thought about that for a moment. "*You* were behind this?"

"I was trying to help. Okay?"

He snorted. "And your grandfather . . . he's the genius who picked out that nag?"

I gave a sheepish nod. "Yeah."

He shot me a look of pure disdain. "Man, I thought your grandpa knew everything there was to know about horses."

"So did I, Amigo," I sighed. "So did I."

Each day after work I'd drop by and we'd sit on the patio and watch the little mare. She had begun to eat, but only when the other horses had finished. Not once during those early days did I see her enter the stables. Every night when I left to go home, she would be standing alone in the corner behind the watering trough. Every morning when Steven got up, that's where she'd still be. If anyone or anything approached the corral she would scamper away, keeping as much distance between herself and the intruder as possible.

One day, I went with Mr. Callister to throw down

95

some hay from the loft. The little mare must have been asleep on her feet. We were almost within touching distance of her before she sensed our presence. Eyes reflecting her terror, she backed away hard, almost breaking through the wire fence. Then in one bold leap, like a jumper in a steeplechase, she cleared the trough and hit dirt on the other side running.

From the patio came a loud guffaw. "She jumps around like a scared cricket!" Steven yelled.

Cricket.

Mr. Callister and I exchanged knowing looks. The little black mare had a name.

A couple of days later I found Steven standing alone at the corral fence with his eyes fixed on Cricket. "Wonder how she got that mangled ear?" he said when I joined him.

"She's a mustang," I said. "See that brand?" There was a cruel, deeply burned scar on the mare's left rump. "That's a stock supply outfit up near Crownpoint. They track the wild herds around Chaco Canyon and cut out a few head every month to sell. Some of those rounders can be pretty mean. They break a mustang's spirit by gouging a steel cable through his ear and tying his head to a post. Then they strap a saddle on him and let him stay that way for days at a time without food, sometimes without water. Makes 'em easier to handle, they claim."

Steven's jaw firmed. "You think that happened to her?"

"She's got all the signs. Horses like that, they've been broken-in the hard way. You can usually ride them, *if* you can saddle then. But getting close enough to do that—that's the trick. This little mare's gonna need a whole lot of TLC to calm her down enough to be ridden."

"Bastards!" he exclaimed. "No wonder she's so

damned scared of everything that moves." I could sense the new-found empathy he felt for a creature so hurt, so alienated, so utterly friendless.

Every day thereafter, that's where I'd find him—at the fence, studying the little mare with a new intensity. She studied him back, cautiously at first. Then, as time passed she began to accept his presence. It was as if she had figured out that he was just as wary of her as she was of him.

One evening he did something that gave me a glimmer of hope. He bent down and pulled up a handful of grass, and held it over the fence. "Hey, Cricket," he called, softly.

The little mare was standing about fifteen feet away. At the sound of his voice she raised her head and cocked her ears forward.

"Come on, little mare. I won't hurt you . . . come on."

I was flabbergasted, and amused. He was talking to her! Once he had told me I was a candidate for the funny farm for talking to horses. I wondered if he remembered that. I decided it didn't matter. What mattered was what was happening now.

Cricket took a couple of hesitant steps toward us, then stopped. I backed away slowly and went to the patio, leaving him alone at the fence. He called her name again, coaxing her. With nervous eyes locked on his outstretched hand, she took a few more steps. I held my breath. Venturing as close as she dared, she extended her neck its full length and nuzzled the tufts of green from his opened fingers, then retreated to her haven behind the water trough to eat it.

"Way to go, Amigo," I called.

Steven pushed back from the fence, beaming.

The experiment continued. One day he gave her a sugar cube, surely a new treat for the once-wild mustang. By the end of a week she was coming to the fence at his call. Wounded horse and wounded boy forged a new friendship founded on mutual alienation and hurts. But it went no further. The fence was always there, always between them.

Then came the day Mr. Callister decided to shoe Cricket.

By then, school had started again. My chores as a *vaquero* had been suspended until next summer. Each morning Steven and I would catch the school bus behind the 7-Eleven Store at Bosque Farms, and each afternoon we'd ride it home. No one complained anymore that I was on the wrong bus—not with Steven at my side. News of his bloody knock-down, drag-out with Bulldog that summer had traveled far. On the bus, and at school, guys treated him with cautious respect. But when the talk turned to bronco busting or rodeoing or the big event, Mr. Cole's upcoming trail ride, Steven would find somewhere else to go, or something else to do.

It was on a Saturday, after school started, that Mr. Callister asked me to help him trim Cricket's hoofs in preparation for shoeing her. "It's gotta be done, they're beginning to split. We're not gonna take any foolishness from her, either." He went to the tack shed and got his lariat.

She was in her usual place behind the trough. When we approached her, one on each side, she snorted and started to sidle. Whichever way she turned, we'd shoo her back. Then she spotted the rope in Mr. Callister's hand and all hell broke loose. He formed a quick loop. "She's spooked!"

Before he could throw, Cricket wheeled about to face the barbed-wire fence. Flexing her range-hard muscles she jumped. She almost cleared the high barrier, but her rear fetlocks caught on the top strand. She crashed to the ground, bringing the fence down with her. She was savagely entangled in sharp wire.

Snorting in terror, she pushed up on her front legs and lunged forward, ripping the steel corner post from its foundation. Strands of taut wire snapped and whipped around her, slicing into her haunches. It would only take a few minutes for her to cut herself to ribbons.

"Get the wire cutters!" Mr. Callister yelled. "I've got to get a rope on her before she strips her legs bare!"

I ran to the tack room and hurried back.

Spying the rope again Cricket slammed herself against the ground, thrashing about in a frantic attempt to tear free. Each move dug the wire deeper and deeper into her flesh. Mr. Callister raised the lariat.

All at once, as if he had materialized from thin air, Steven was there. Slipping between his father and me he approached the enraged and frightened horse.

"Steven!" Mr. Callister shouted and reached for him. "Stop!"

Evading his father's outstretched arm, Steven walked up and put his hand on Cricket's face. "Okay, little mare . . . okay, now . . . it'll be all right." Softly, gently, he talked to her, all the while stroking her face and neck.

For an agonizing moment she froze, barely breathing, like a desperate person poised on a high ledge unsure whether to leap or live. Then she exhaled a shuddering moan and lay back, quiet.

Steven reached back. "The rope," he whispered.

His father laid the lariat in his hand. Steven eased the noose up over Cricket's head and neck and drew it snug. Mr. Callister took the cutters from me, went behind the mare and snipped the barbed wire from her legs.

99

"Can you get her up?" Mr. Callister asked.

Steven tugged lightly at the rope. Cricket raised her head and pushed up on her front legs. She remained that way for several seconds. Again he coaxed her. All at once she stood, shook herself briskly and stepped free of the tangled fence. With one hand on the rope and the other caressing her neck, Steven led her through the pasture to the rear gate and back into the corral.

I started to follow but Mr. Callister put a restraining hand on my shoulder. "Let's go to the house."

We retreated to the patio.

Steven stayed with Cricket. I watched from the glider as he washed her and treated her wounds, then fed and watered her and rubbed her down.

In the days that followed, driven by his compassion for the hurt mare, he did all that was necessary for Cricket, alone.

But he still refused to ride.

Chapter 13

The phone call that would change our lives came at midnight. Roused from a deep sleep, I heard Papa go to the kitchen to answer. Moments later he voiced an oath and called Mama. Curiosity aroused, I threw off the cover and grabbed my pants.

When I got to the kitchen Papa was putting on his clothes. Mama was packing sandwiches and perking coffee for the thermos. Papa saw me. "Tino's pens were busted up again tonight. Young bull killed, two heifers gone."

There was no need to explain. Since that day on the mesa when Tino had put a bullet in Diablo's shoulder the old bull had avoided the valley. Now he'd come down from the mountains to raise hell again. Was it coincidence that his victim was the man who had shot him?

Papa tugged at his boots. "Last time he was spotted was in August—in the ponderosa grove up above Burnt Tree Canyon. Tino figures that's his lair now, that he's headed back up there." Papa pushed his pant legs down over his boot tops, got up and went to the bedroom and came back carrying his lever-action Winchester .44–40 and a box of shells. He worked the lever a couple of times then poured the shells in his

101

jacket pocket. His intent was written all over his face, and it meant breaking pueblo law.

"Papa," I started to warn him, "the pueblo council . . ."

"Can go straight to hell," he said, firmly. "Tino and I aim to settle scores once and for all."

I started for my room. "I'm going too."

He stopped me. "No. We might be gone a couple of days. You stay in school. Take care of things here 'til I get back."

"But, Papa."

"No buts, David."

I knew that tone. There was no use arguing further. I nodded.

His voice softened. "Good. Now don't worry . . . either of you."

He cradled the rifle in the crook of his arm, grabbed the sack of sandwiches and the thermos, then left.

I was too wired to think of sleep. "It's not fair," I complained.

Mama took down a pan and heated some milk. She filled two cups and handed one to me. "He's doing what he thinks best."

"I could help . . . I wouldn't be in the way."

"I know."

We drank the milk. After a while, I calmed down. Mama stood and put the cups in the sink. "Let's go to bed, David. You still have chores before school."

I slept fitfully, tormented by a nightmare of Papa face-to-face with a murderous *corriente* bull.

"David!" I thought the voice was part of my dream. A hand shook my shoulder. The voice was more urgent. "David . . . wake up!" It was Mama. *Chore time already?* I glanced at the clock. 2:05 A.M.

Mama was at the window. I heard Sundance

whinny. I jumped out of bed, and went to the window and froze. In the pasture behind the corral, grimly illuminated by the light from a chalk-white moon, stood Diablo! The wily bull had fooled us all. Instead of returning to the mountain, he had backtracked through the flats and crossed the shallow river onto our property.

Why? We had no heifers for him to add to his harem, no young bulls for him to challenge. Then it came to me. *Sundance*! Sometime during the night, Diablo had caught the scent of an old enemy. He had followed it here to seek revenge.

Using his head for a battering ram, the old bull lunged at the corral fence. Twisting and gouging with his single horn, he ripped the wire from the posts. Sundance reared and pawed the air in panic.

I had to do something. My mind raced . . . *Papa's gun cabinet*!

I pushed back from the window and ran down the hall to my parent's room. My father's heavy oak gun cabinet stood against the wall beside the bed. It was locked! I grabbed one of Papa's shoes off the floor and broke the glass pane and opened the cabinet door. I looked for the Winchester. Then I remembered. Papa had taken it. "Damn!"

Papa's Browning 12-gauge pump shotgun lay across the top rack. He let me use it that summer to hunt ring-neck pheasants that nested along the irrigation ditches. It would be almost useless against Diablo. But it was all I had. I grabbed the shotgun and rummaged through the bottom drawer. The gun was plugged to take only three shells. I found a box of Federal, number six shot, and loaded three of them into the gun. I pumped a round into the chamber and ran out the back door.

By now the corral fence was a jumble of wire and

wooden posts, scattered on the ground. Disentangling himself from the clutter, Diablo entered the enclosure. Sundance cowered in the far corner. I rushed to the gate at the front of the corral, steadied the Browning atop it, took aim and fired. The blast resounded through the night. Diablo thrashed his head twice as the lead shots peppered him. It was about as effective as a BB gun.

Thoroughly enraged now, Diablo turned to confront the new menace. Cocking his good eye to catch my silhouette in the moonlight, he started toward the gate. Heart in my throat, I backed away. I pumped a new round in the chamber and fired again. Diablo tossed his head, shrugging off the pellets as if they were no more than a minor irritation. When he reached the gate, he lowered his head and kept coming. The gate splintered like a sapling falling before a Sherman tank.

Diablo was now in the barren yard, just behind our house. Still in retreat, I pumped the final round into the chamber. Just then my foot hit something and I stumbled backward. The gun flew out of my hands. I sat on the ground, dazed.

Ten feet in front of me, Diablo lowered his head and pawed the ground. I heard someone scream ''*David*!'' and a blurred form rushed past me. It was Mama! She pulled the axe out of the chopping block I'd stumbled over, raised it above her head and took a stand between me and the killer bull.

Frantic now, I looked around for the gun. I spotted it in the dirt, six feet off to my right. There was no time to get to my feet. I crawled for the gun. ''Mama! Jump aside!''

Diablo began his charge.

I lifted the gun and fired point blank at the onrushing bull. With a furious bellow he wheeled to face the corral and stood deathly still. I ran to Mama and pulled her back toward the house. Grandpa and Miguel were standing in the doorway, their faces masks of fear.

"Miguel!" I yelled. "Papa's gun cabinet . . . shotgun shells . . . quick!"

Miguel took off for Papa's bedroom.

I took the axe from Mama. "Mama! Go inside!"

She refused to leave me.

As if frozen in time, Diablo stood without moving. After what seemed an eternity he lifted his head to the moonlit sky, emitted another blood-curdling bellow and started ripping the ground with his hoof. In a moment he would turn around to complete the murderous business he'd come for. *Where was Miguel*?

I raised the axe.

Suddenly the night was filled with sounds of racing trucks and shouts of alarm. I knew at once what it meant. Neighbors who'd heard my shots were coming to investigate.

"Mama! Hear!" I cried aloud, but remained poised with the axe.

Mama crossed herself. "*Gracias . . . gracias*," she whispered in a trembling voice.

The clamor grew closer. Diablo stopped pawing. Without looking back, the old bull took off in a lumbering gallop toward the river.

Clinging to each other, Mama and I watched until he vanished into the night.

Chapter 14

I rapped on the glass.

No response.

I rapped harder, then again.

A bedside lamp came on.

There was a pole-mounted vapor light on that side of the house. I stepped back into the illumination. After a startled yelp of recognition, Steven got up and raised the window. "Hey, man . . . you realize what time it is? What the hell . . . ?"

"Three-thirty." I kept my voice low, so as not to awaken his parents. "Meet me out front. I gotta talk to you."

He rubbed sleep from his eyes and gave me a "you crazy?" look. Something in my face must have convinced him. He grabbed his pants and a pair of slippers and left the room.

Moments later he came out the front door zipping his pants. He crossed the yard to the hitching post, where I was standing beside Sundance. "All right . . . what's so damned important to get a guy outa bed this time of night?" His voice was still edgy.

I told him about Diablo and what had happened that night, in detail. "Mama sent me to get Papa. But I'm not going. I'm going after that Devil." I pointed to

106

the shotgun in the saddle scabbard. "That pea-shooter ain't worth Diddley. I need your dad's rifle."

In the semi-darkness I could see the fear and awe that vied for control of his countenance. "I . . . I don't know. Look, we went after that crazy bull once, and . . . well, you said yourself you aren't a real *vaquero* yet . . . Your mom's right . . . go find your dad . . . he'll know what to do . . ."

He went on like that, talking a mile a minute, almost pleading, trying to hit on an argument that might dissuade me.

I cut him off. "My mom's also an Apache, Amigo. I think *she'd* know what to do too, if she had the chance. Look . . . all I'm asking for is the loan of your dad's rifle and some ammo. I know how to use it."

He began to shake his head. "It's a scope sight. No good in the dark."

"I'm gonna stake out. If he's high-tailin' it to where I think he is, he's gonna have to pass through that dry arroyo up by Running Bear piñon before he gets to Burnt Tree Canyon, where Papa and Tino are waiting for him. I'm gonna beat them to him and cut him off at Running Bear. There'll be plenty of light for a scope sight at sunup."

He didn't comment.

"Amigo"—I put all the conviction I could muster into my voice—"I'm gonna take that bull down before he succeeds in killing someone." I patted the sheathed shotgun. "If I have to face him with this, that's the way it'll have to be. But, one way or another, *I'm gonna do it.*"

He studied my face a moment. Then without a word he turned and went into the house. Minutes later he came out carrying his father's .30–06 bolt-action Winchester and a clip of shells. He thrust the ammo at me. "Two-hundred grain, lead nose. They'll do the job . . . if you can shoot straight."

"I can shoot straight."

He held the rifle out to me. "The scope's dead on at twenty-five yards. Set it myself. Beyond that you'll have to use Kentucky windage. And watch the trigger . . . it's a hard pull."

I took the gun. "Thanks. I mean that."

"Save it. I'm not sure I'm doing you any favors."

I loaded the clip into the rifle, leaving the chamber empty. Then I pulled the shotgun out of the scabbard, handed it to Steven, and shoved the rifle in its place. I climbed into the saddle.

Steven grabbed the cinch strap. "Look, Dave . . . you sure you know what you're doing? I mean . . . you can't tell about that tricky bastard."

"I'm sure. For Papa, for you, for what he almost did to Mama and me tonight. I'm sure." I clinched the reins in one hand and gave him a farewell salute with the other. *"Adios*, Amigo."

I kicked Sundance in the flanks and headed for the river.

The trail along the backside of the Callister Ranch led to the flats. I had no intention of riding through that foreboding Olive tree grove in the darkness. Way I figured, that's where Diablo would hole up until dawn. I could skirt the flats to the north and still be at Running Bear inside of an hour. That would leave another hour or more before first light, plenty of time to get settled for what had to be done.

A half-hour from the Callister Ranch, the strong aroma of rotting algae told me I'd reached the stagnant pools where Steven and I had hogged carp what now seemed like a million years ago. Not far beyond the pools I entered the cottonwood grove that bordered the flats. Soft moonlight filtered through the foliage, casting eerie shadows along the trail. In that mellow glow, I could make out the fallen tree trunk where Steven, Brenda and I had rested following our harrowing first meeting with Diablo that February day seven months ago. Barely a month later, on my fifteenth birthday, my father was gored. The next day, trying to help me reap revenge, my best friend was shattered in body and spirit. Papa . . . Steven. Victims of the same crazed menace. The thought spurred me on.

I had just cleared the cottonwoods and turned eastward onto the climbing trail to Black Mesa, when I heard them. Hoofbeats, faint and in the distance, but approaching. *Pueblo mounted patrol*? Surely they'd question me, a fifteen-year-old boy armed with a high-powered rifle, far north of the direction I should be riding to alert my father. They'd make me return home, maybe even escort me to the pueblo police station. I wheeled Sundance about and spurred him down the ditch bank into a clump of Olive trees.

The hoofbeats grew louder. Two riders? I concentrated on the rhythm. It was only one, coming toward me fast. That was strange. The mounted police always patrolled in pairs.

The rider emerged from the cottonwood grove and turned at a gallop onto the Black Mesa trail. Just then Sundance snorted. I leaned forward and grasped his nostrils. ''Shh-h-h!''

Too late. The rider reined to a stop and looked from side to side. Above, on the high bank, he loomed like a ghostly phantom silhouetted against the autumn moon. Small mount . . . tall rider. Then his face caught the light. *My God*!

I spurred Sundance up the bank.

''Wha . . . ?'' the rider recoiled in alarm and wheeled to face me.

I reined up right in front of him. I tried to speak, but emotion choked back the words before they could leave my mouth. I could only utter "*Madre de Dios . . . Madre de Dios*" over and over. Hot tears stung my cheeks. They were tears of joy, relief, thanksgiving. I wondered if he could see them.

We sat there like that for several minutes, neither of us speaking, each of us reading in silence what was in the other's heart. After a while Steven lifted Cricket's reins and turned again toward Black Mesa.

"Amigo," he said, "let's go hunt a bull."

Chapter 15

I turned up the collar of my denim jacket and eyed Steven's wool mackinaw with envy. "Man, I wish I'd brought some coffee." I rubbed my hands together briskly.

"Yeah," Steven agreed.

We were hunkered down in a ravine on high Black Mesa just below Running Bear piñon. Visible twenty miles to the north, ever-sprawling Albuquerque was awakening to the rays of a new-day sun, beaming through Tijeras Canyon. But here, in the shadow of the Manzanos, it would be another quarter hour at least before there would be enough light for us to have a clear view of the mesa between us and the flats.

"You really believe he's down there?" Steven asked.

"You bet. He always holes up in the flats overnight before heading for the mountains."

"That's a lot of territory. We just gonna wait him out?"

"Yeah. Makes no difference where he comes out, he's still gotta head up through that arroyo over there. If he doesn't show in an hour or so, I'll ride down and lure him out."

"*We'll* ride down and lure him out," Steven said.

Something about that made my stomach churn. Déjà vu. Visions of Steven lying broken and bleeding on this very mesa ran through my mind. "Look, Amigo . . . you being here with me . . . riding again. I know what that took. And . . . well, it's a good feeling, you know . . . you doin' that for me. But this is my fight."

"Bull."

"No. No bull." I said firmly. I tried to lighten it by adding, "Besides, man . . . I got the gun."

"And I got the scars."

It was hard to argue with that, but I tried. I nodded toward where the horses were tied. "I can tell you've been working with Cricket. You couldn't have gotten her up here otherwise. But she's still awful spooky. That could be dangerous."

"Not with me, she ain't. And don't sell her short. She's no Cheyenne, but we're not tie-fasting today. Besides, she's quick. She could run three circles around that *corriente* before Cheyenne ever got going."

His mind was made up. "Guess there's no use arguing then."

"Right, there's no use arguing."

I punched him on the shoulder. "Amigo, it's good to have you back."

The sky was turning orange. In another few minutes the long shadows would yield to a new dawn. In that waning twilight I leaned back against the bank and studied my friend. On this fateful night, he too had emerged from the shadows that had engulfed his life. It was indeed a new day. Building on that thought I said, "So, guess you'll be going on the trail ride next week."

"Guess so," he said, and from his tone I knew it wasn't a sudden thought.

"Know who's starting the races that day?"

112

"Frank James," he replied, with a mocking laugh. I'd told him the story.

"Close," I said. "Grandpa."

"Your grandfather? Well I'll be damned." He thought about that for a moment. "You know, I'm sorry . . . what I said about him, I mean. He does know about horses, doesn't he?"

"Yeah. Horses and . . . lots more besides."

We were silent a moment, then I asked, "You takin' Brenda?"

"I'm gonna ask her."

"Then you'll be taking her," I assured him, knowing that it was the beginning of new and better things between them.

He asked, "How 'bout you? Rosie?"

"You better believe."

He chuckled. "Gonna find out the truth about her yet, huh?"

It conjured the memory of that day on the bank at the carp pool when we'd rolled in the dry grass and pondered the mystery of girls. "Hey, Amigo," I returned the chuckle, "have I not always been a seeker of truth?"

We both laughed all the harder.

At full light I went to Sundance and retrieved the Winchester from the saddle scabbard. Then I went to the crest of the bank, took a prone position and looked down over the mesa. Steven lay down by my side and pushed his Stetson back on his head. From this altitude we could see the flats, all the way from Bosque Farms on the north to Los Lunas on the south. A half-mile downhill was the grove of Russian Olive trees from which Diablo had emerged that day in March to challenge us. In the crystal-clear New Mexico air it appeared much closer.

"Right down there's where you roped him," I said.

113

"Yeah."

We didn't expand on that.

The ancient cattle trail that wound its way from the flats was in full light now. If Diablo was lurking down there in the trees—and I was positive he was—he'd take that trail on his way to the mountains. At its closest, the trail passed within a hundred yards of where we lay, with nothing but open mesa between.

"Broadside shot," Steven said. "Easy pickin's."

I agreed. "Look, you want first crack at him? You got every right."

"No," he declined. " 'Course, if you miss, I'll finish the job."

"Hah!"

Time passed. The sun rose ever higher in its climb above the Manzanos, bringing steadily increasing temperatures. From a distant valley came the churning sounds of the old windmill that fed the tank where Steven and I once took an impromptu swim. High overhead, an eastbound jetliner spun a wispy silver contrail in the azure sky. There was no sign of Diablo.

"What time is it?" I asked for the dozenth time.

Steven glanced at his wrist. "Eight-ten."

"Damn it. He should be out by now."

"If he's down there."

"Yeah," I said, giving way to doubt. I shaded my eyes and scanned the tree-line from one end of the flats to the other. Nothing.

"Think we oughta ride down?" Steven asked.

I pondered it, suddenly aware of how very tired I was. The nervous energy, the adrenaline that had kept me going through the night, was beginning to wear off. "Few more minutes, okay? If he don't show by eight-thirty, we'll go down and drive him out."

"Okay."

I gave a hard yawn and laid my head on my forearm.

114

"David!"

The voice was urgent, far away.

"David! Wake up!"

"Huh?" I rubbed the sleep from my eyes and looked around. Steven was down in the ravine, running in a low crouch toward the other side.

"What?" I called after him. Then I heard the commotion. Sundance and Cricket . . . snorting in alarm and tugging at their tethers. In a frenzy, Sundance reared, almost slipping his bridle.

On the far side of the ravine Steven dropped prone on the ground and raised his head just enough to see over the embankment. "David! The gun! Quick!"

I grabbed the rifle, raced across the ravine and dropped beside Steven. His face was ashen. I peeked over the bank. Forty yards away, heading straight for us, was Diablo.

"It's crazy!" I blurted. "He *always* takes the trail . . . he's never come up the backside . . ."

"Man"—Steven's voice was shrill—"this ain't no time for a history lesson. Get a round in that chamber, fast!"

I jumped to my knees and yanked the bolt back then shoved it hard forward, seating a round into the firing chamber. My thoughts raced. There could be only one explanation for this ominous turn of events. Diablo had turned the tables. *He* was stalking *us*. He must have caught our scent and circled the ravine to ambush us from behind. Why else would the wily bull be climbing the steep, boulder-strewn north slope rather than taking the traditional trail? If it hadn't been for the horses sounding the alarm, he might have pulled it off.

I raised the gun to my shoulder and waited. In a moment Diablo would stop, lower his head and begin ripping the earth with his hoof. At that instant, while he was standing still, I'd put a bullet through his brain.

Dangerously close now, the bull dropped his head almost to the ground. But, instead of stopping, he forged onward.

Sundance and Cricket were going crazy. Steven emitted an oath. "For God's sake, man . . . give me the damned rifle!"

I released the safety and fixed my eye to the scope. Less than twenty yards away now, the bull's head loomed through the glass four times life-size. An icy tremor shot up my spine. It was as if I could reach out and touch that rapier-sharp horn. Remembering what my father had taught me about shooting, I sucked in a deep breath, slowly released some of it, and centered the cross-hairs in the middle of that massive head. I started to squeeze the trigger.

Then I saw it.

"Shoot, man . . . *Shoot*!"

I sat back on my heels and held the gun out to Steven.

He yanked it from my hands and threw it to his shoulder and took aim.

I waited.

He didn't fire.

"Well I'll be damned," he said. He lowered the gun and pushed the safety back on.

I took the gun again and fixed the scope once more on Diablo's head. Where the bull's demonic right eye had been, there was now only a bloody socket. What remained of the eye dangled from his mutilated face in a matted glob of festering tissue. From the peppered pattern on his head, there was no question what had caused the wounds. My final shotgun blast last night had found its mark. Diablo was totally blind.

Steven spoke first. "Looks like you already got your revenge."

"Yeah . . . looks that way." I wondered why I didn't feel better about it.

"Where's he going?"

"Home."

We got to our feet as Diablo stumbled on. Fifteen feet from us he raised his head and flared his nostrils, catching now the full impact of our scent. He stopped. I released the safety and held the gun ready. With a mighty shake of his head the old bull turned what was left of his face toward us and let out a long mournful bellow. It was as if he was telling us that the game was over. Then, head almost dragging the ground, he turned to continue the treacherous climb toward the high Manzanos.

"Think he'll he make it?" Steven asked.

"He'll make it," I replied, understanding the force that was driving the blind bull onward.

"He'll only starve to death."

I shook my head. "No. He's easy prey now for every puma on the hunt, every younger bull with a grudge against him. They'll kill him long before he has a chance to starve."

"Well that's just plain stupid. Why's he going back up there, then?"

"He's like my people," I explained. "He's going home, to die where he was born."

From the look on Steven's face I knew he was giving that some serious thought. He removed his Stetson and slapped it hard against his still-healing leg. "Damn it!" His voice was filled with emotion. "Why do I feel so . . . so *sorry* for him?"

"I don't know," I said, with equal passion. "I just . . . don't know."

After a while Steven shoved the hat back on his head. "We better go calm the horses."

"Yeah," I agreed. "Guess we better."

We rode downhill in silence, each deep in his own private thoughts. At the north end of the olive trees, where the mesa trail turned toward the ditch trail, Steven stopped, reined around and gazed back toward the mountains. I did the same. Far in the distance, a mere dot now in the vast foothills of the Manzanos, Diablo was continuing his final climb homeward.

I watched for a moment then reined back toward the flats. "C'mon, Amigo. There's an anxious, blue-eyed redhead down there waiting for you to ask her for a date."

It was the right thing to say. Steven reined about with a smile. "And there's a frisky brown-eyed brunette down there waiting for you to seek the truth."

"Ha!" I took tight grip on the reins. "Race you to the cottonwood grove, Amigo."

He beamed at the challenge. "Loser cleans the other's stables."

"You're on," I agreed.

"HI-AY-E-EE-E!" he yelled, and spurred Cricket on.

"HI-AY-E-EE-E!" I repeated, and spurred Sundance after him.

I didn't care who got to the cottonwoods first.

We had both already won.

NOVELS FROM AVON FLARE

CLASS PICTURES	61408-1/$2.95 US/$3.50 Can

Marilyn Sachs

Pat, always the popular one, and shy, plump Lolly have been best friends since kindergarten, through thick and thin, supporting each other during crises. But everything changes when Lolly turns into a thin, pretty blonde and Pat finds herself playing second fiddle for the first time.

BABY SISTER	70358-1/$3.50 US/$4.25 Can

Marilyn Sachs

Her sister was everything Penny could never be, until Penny found something else.

THE GROUNDING OF GROUP 6	83386-7/$3.25 US/$3.75 Can

Julian Thompson

What do parents do when they realize that their sixteen-year old son or daughter is a loser and an embarrassment to the family? Five misfits find they've been set up to disappear at exclusive Coldbrook School, but aren't about to allow themselves to be permanentaly "grounded."

TAKING TERRI MUELLER	79004-1/$3.50 US/$4.25 Can

Norma Fox Mazer

Was it possible to be kidnapped by your own father? Terri's father has always told her that her mother died in a car crash—but now Terri has reason to suspect differently, and she struggles to find the truth on her own.

RECKLESS	83717-X/$2.95 US/$3.50 Can

Jeanette Mines

It was Jeannie Tanger's first day of high school when she met Sam Benson. Right from the beginning—when he nicknamed her JT—they were meant for each other. But right away there was trouble; family trouble; school trouble—could JT save Sam from himself?

FLARE NOVELS BY
Ellen Emerson White

FRIENDS FOR LIFE 82578-3/$2.95 U.S./$3.50 Can.
A heart-wrenching mystery about Susan McAllister, a
high school senior whose best friend dies—supposedly
of a drug overdose. Her efforts to clear her friend's
reputation and identify the killer bring her closer to the
truth—and danger.

THE PRESIDENT'S DAUGHTER
88740-1/$2.95 U.S./$3.50 Can.
When Meg's mother runs for President—and wins—
Meg's life becomes anything but ordinary.

ROMANCE IS A WONDERFUL THING
83907-5/$2.95 U.S./$3.50 Can.
Trish Masters, honor student and all-around preppy, falls
in love with Colin McNamara—the class clown. As their
relationship grows, Trish realizes that if she can give Colin
the confidence to show his true self to the world, their
romance *can* be a wonderful thing.

WHITE HOUSE AUTUMN
89780-6/$2.95 U.S./$3.25 Can.
In the sequel to THE PRESIDENT'S DAUGHTER,
Meg struggles to lead a normal life as the daughter of the
first woman President of the United States.